BREAKING KNEES
SIXTY-THREE
VERY SHORT STORIES
FROM SYRIA
ZAKARIA TAMER
TRANSLATED FROM THE ARABIC BY IBRAHIM MUHAWI

BREAKING KNEES
SIXTY-THREE
VERY SHORT STORIES
FROM SYRIA
ZAKARIA TAMER
TRANSLATED FROM THE ARABIC BY IBRAHIM MUHAWI

periscope
www.periscopebooks.co.uk

Breaking Knees
Sixty-three Very Short Stories from Syria

This edition published in 2016 in Great Britain by

Periscope
An imprint of Garnet Publishing Limited
8 Southern Court, South Street
Reading RG1 4QS

www.periscopebooks.co.uk
www.facebook.com/periscopebooks
www.twitter.com/periscopebooks
www.instagram.com/periscope_books
www.pinterest.com/periscope

1 2 3 4 5 6 7 8 9 10

ISBN 9781902932453

A CIP catalogue record for this book is available from the British Library.

This book has been typeset using Periscope UK,
a font created specially for this imprint.

Typeset by Samantha Barden
Jacket design by James Nunn: www.jamesnunn.co.uk

Printed and bound in Lebanon by International Press:
interpress@int-press.com

ACKNOWLEDGMENTS

A Lannan Foundation residency (in Marfa, Texas) gave me the opportunity to start work on this translation during the summer of 2004. I am happy to acknowledge the contribution of the Foundation and its staff to the welfare of this project. Martha Jessup provided intellectual support and Douglas Humble looked after my welfare while in Marfa. The work was finished with the support of the International Center for Writing and Translation at the University of California, Irvine. I am grateful to the Center for the award of one of its 2006–2007 translations grants, and to Professors Ammiel Alcalay, James Monroe, and Yasir Suleiman for their recommendations. Rick London and Sid Gershgoren read parts of the manuscript and offered many valuable suggestions. The unqualified support of Dan Nunn of Garnet Publishing was essential to the process of publication.

The contribution of my wife Jane Muhawi (whom in a previous acknowledgement I called "my native ear") is more than can be put into words. Her superb command of the language and her ear for nuance have boosted my confidence in producing a translation that (I feel) does justice to the Arabic original.

Ibrahim Muhawi

INTRODUCTION

Zakaria Tamer (b. 1931 in Damascus) is acknowledged as one of the great writers of the modern Arab world. His writing covers a range of literary forms, including stories for children and satirical reflections on Arab affairs that first appeared as newspaper columns and were later collected into separate volumes. His literary stature and influence, however, rest on the type of very short story (*al-qissa al-qasira jiddan*) included in this work. The first volume of these (*Neighing of the White Stallion*) came out in 1960 and this work, which is the tenth, in 2002 under the title *Taksir Rukab* (*Breaking Knees*). The eleventh, *The Hedgehog: A Story* (2005), is a set of twenty-two tales that recount the experiences of a single character, a highly imaginative child. Tamer's fecund imagination and his unique and productive pen will not allow him to rest on his laurels. The next volume of stories is already in the making, and I'm sure others (as well as the stream of newspaper columns) will follow for as long as he lives.

Tamer has often been referred to as a master of the short story, but this is not an entirely accurate description. True, the (very) short story is his preferred form, but he hardly ever publishes these separately. His usual practice is to publish a collection as a single work revolving around a set of themes. The fact that Tamer subtitles *The Hedgehog* "a story," though composed of twenty-two individual tales, is clear indication that he wishes us to read his books as artistic units. We see this process at work in the present volume as well, where the stories do not have names but numbers. This is an important point to bear in mind while reading *Breaking Knees*. Each story can stand on its own, yet there are underlying (and frequently quite subtle) connections of theme, style, and perspective that knit the work together in the reader's mind long after the book has been read. Actually, the format of the book encourages frequent reading. The work is too intense to be read at one sitting, but the seemingly endless inventiveness in plot and the underlying humor of the writing will keep readers curious as to what the author will be up to next.

Tamer is a satirist, and the target of his satire is the Arab world – its culture, politics, social practices, and dominant religion. In case we have any doubts about what he is doing, he himself tells us directly. To a collection of short essays written at various times but published in 2003 he has given the title *The Victim Satirizes His Killer: Short Essays*. The title tells it all, the victim being the citizen; the killer, the state; and the literary mode, satire. The comment on the back cover of the book declares its intention. It says in part: "Countries in which there is no room for criticism are poor and miserable, worthy of being lambasted, lamented, and held up to ridicule . . . This book . . . is a modest attempt to offer some criticism of all that holds people down and retards their development and their enjoyment of their right to a life free of fear . . ."

The general theme of *Breaking Knees*, as of much of Tamer's work, is repression: of the individual by the institutions of state and religion and of individuals by each other, particularly women by men. Thus the question of authority – political, social, sexual, and religious – forms the thematic core of the book, with (female) sexuality receiving the lion's share of concern. Political authority is manifest in the emphasis in many stories on the machinations of the police state – arbitrary arrest and detention, interrogations, corruption. Social authority expresses itself in the patriarchal cultural order and the dominance of religious and cultural institutions and conventions that constrain individual freedom. Many stories stress religious hypocrisy and the unfulfilled sexual expectations of women. In some the marriage bed is associated with a place of death for women. *Breaking Knees* is a daring work of art that deals with taboo subjects like religion and female sexuality in a frank manner and expresses an urgently felt need for change.

In bringing together religion, politics, and sexuality (sometimes all three in the same story) the author is telling us indirectly that these forms of oppression are all connected. There is a malaise at the core of the traditional Arab psyche, perhaps at the core of Arab culture itself, that accounts for the aberrant behavior of many of many of Tamer's characters. From the perspective of the countless Arab individuals who have adopted modern values based on democratic institutions and human rights, a state of affairs characterized by political and cultural stagnation, destructive worship of tradition, and glorification of a mythical past, appears truly dire. To understand Tamer's satiric method and the complexity of his narrative vision, we have to put his work in the context of this malaise.

It would be a mistake, of course, to focus solely on the activist, political aspect of these stories at the expense of appreciating them as literature – that is, as discourse that through the particular reaches for the universal. Tamer extends the boundaries of what is possible in fiction. His art is based on a radical questioning of what is usually taken to be "reality" in a work of fiction. His work alerts us to the extent that we as readers come to any story armed with a set of assumptions about the protocols of narrative, such as plot, character, continuity, plausibility, and probability. All these conventions are challenged, and frequently broken. Those who read fiction for comfort must prepare to be shocked at this unrelenting assault on their expectations. Tamer's fictional world often draws on the world of the dream to confuse the boundaries of the real and the imagined, or even the boundary between life and death: a house can be a character, so can an apple, a cat, a statue, a dead (or seemingly dead) person, as well as the angels and the jinn. Temporality in his stories does not always conform to the ordinary perception of the forward movement of time: a character's life, for example, may not necessarily end with his or her death. Characters who have died, or ghost-like characters who can only be described as the living dead, continue to exercise a palpable influence on the world of the living.

Though this surreal world is rather rare in written fiction, it characterizes the animistic and mythological world of the folktale (the universal form of narrative par excellence) where everything has a voice and can speak, where time is indeterminate, and space has flexible boundaries. The natural world is suffused with the supernatural, and what takes place does not necessarily conform to expectations. The purpose of fantasy and wonder in folktales is to appeal to the imagination of children, which is more active than that of adults. Tamer draws on the childhood experience of orally recited tales to challenge our comfortable accommodation with the world. The pleasure of reading these stories will be heightened if readers remain alert to the ways in which they touch base with the art of the oral tales, especially the manner in which folktales transform the world of ordinary perception into that of the imagination.

In this work the universal takes many forms, the most important being the theme of gender identity and conflict, a ubiquitous subject in literature going all the way back to the myth of the Garden of Eden. The opening allegory of the book (itself a major literary form in all literature) announces this theme. Perhaps the patriarchal social order that prevails in most Arab countries gives the subject of gender identity and conflict an additional poignancy, but its significance for literature in general arises from its reach into practically all aspects of life, from the level of personal identity to that of social interaction and culturally determined modes of behavior. From this great subject arise subsidiary themes that endow literature with a moral dimension. I am thinking here of passion, desire, identity, and love of self which animate much individual behavior in these stories.

There are no wasted words in Tamer's musical prose. His descriptions, whether of the environment or of his characters, are always precise and to the point. Since these stories are very short, the writer must get to the action immediately by setting his scenes in familiar environments, like the home, the coffee house, the fields, an orchard, or the street. Though very short the stories are not incomplete. Each offers a psychological portrait that does not challenge credibility. The author does this by means of a number of devices. I have already alluded to a reversal of the relationship between the "real" and the "fictional," yet Tamer uses reversal in a number of other ways as well. He may aim to shock or demonstrate the absurdity of social or gender roles by reversing them. The most shocking for a male-oriented culture would be the reversal of the masculine and feminine that occurs in several stories, with men consciously assuming or being forced into roles and positions usually assigned to women. Sometimes reversal is subtly introduced within the texture of the writing itself when the narrative point of view shifts without warning from the subjective to the objective, allowing more than one voice to speak within the same sentence. The embedded voice, the voice within the voice, also acts like a story within the story, giving us more than one narrative in each story. While the presence of these multiple voices adds psychological depth to the narrative, it also serves to alienate readers from a comfortable relationship with the text, because there is no single voice that speaks through it. The devices I have just mentioned, along with a highly imaginative reliance on metaphor, give these stories a unique form of psychological realism which I call the realism of gesture.

The satirical mode itself also gives this work a universal dimension, for when successfully practiced satire functions within the framework of a sophisticated world literary culture. There may be a problem with contemporary Arab culture and the Arab political system, but literature has always been highly valued by the Arab people, and Arabic literature, though not so well-known in the "West," forms one of the world's great literary traditions, with a history that goes back to well before the rise of Islam in the early seventh century C.E. Historically satire (hija') has been responsible for some of the greatest works of Arabic literature. Yet satirical fiction does not work on its own: it needs irony, which is another universal mode of organizing literary discourse. Irony lightens the air of seriousness by putting some distance between the author and his words. Without irony, which introduces a subtle undertone of wonder into the writing, a satirical author might sound like a moralizer and end up losing the reader. At the same time irony introduces another level of complexity in the narrative voice. If we compare irony to counterpoint in music, then we can see how it acts in concert with Tamer's narrative to enable him to speak in more than one voice at the same time. In Tamer's work we have to see the beauty in the pattern, where we find themes and variations everywhere we turn. The logic of each set of variations is a kind of dialog between what is possible and what is not possible once the assumptions underlying the opening actions are granted.

Tamer is a great prose stylist of the Arabic language, and here is where the challenge in translating him lies. His prose is poetic in its economy – lucid syntax, characterized by precision in the choice of words coupled with sentences that are very much aware of their rhythms. In a novel, or in more conventional short stories, even if the translation suffers from lapses, the translator can always rely on the fictional element to get the meaning across. But Tamer's stories, as I have tried to show here briefly, represent a perfect union of meaning and form in which the performative role of language is part of the satirical meaning. A translation that is not aware of these values and does not make sufficient effort to transfer them to English will, in my opinion, do more harm than good. The choice of words must be managed in such a way that their range of signification always remains under reasonable control, with – if possible – no proliferation of nuances. Each word must be absolutely the right word for the context, and, equally importantly, the rhythm of the prose must dance in English as it does in Arabic. I have tried my best to replicate these values in English. The challenge was to produce an idiomatic and fluent rendering that is sensitive to the sound values of English yet remains as close to the literal meaning of the original as possible. I have therefore aimed for a text that is transparent enough to allow readers to peek through to the original, while at the same time remaining fluent enough to help them forget that what they are reading is a translation. I paid very careful attention to the rhythm of the prose with its measured and nuanced repetition of adjectives, which I have reproduced – sometimes sacrificing fluency for their sake – because repetition is one of the hallmarks of an elegant Arabic prose style. Yet it was not always possible to maintain the rhythmic repetition at the level of the clause, but even here all changes in rhythm were kept to an absolute minimum.

Tamer has been translated into a number of languages (English, German, Russian, Serbian, and Spanish), but he is not as well-known among international readers as he deserves to be, given his achievement. In English he is represented principally by *Tigers on the Tenth Day And Other Stories* (1985), which consists of twenty-four stories that were selected by the translator but which did *not* originally appear together in a single volume. It is my hope that a fresh translation of a recent complete work based on the principles mentioned above will help open a space for Tamer among the reading public in the English-speaking world, encouraging others to translate more of this superb and highly imaginative body of work.

Ibrahim Muhawi, Eugene, OR (USA)

1

The rains were scant. People appealed for help to a saintly man whose prayers were often heard, and a strange, heavy rain fell such as had not been seen before. One drop falling on a man made that which men have, but not women, grow bigger. And one drop falling on a woman made her breasts and buttocks swell. Women were happy, for the real thing was not like the artificial, and cosmetic surgery was very expensive. Men celebrated this correction, which made a trunk out of a branch, but some were not content with what they got for free. They asked for a rain that taught proper manners to any man stupid enough to think that size exempted him from having to rise for a woman.

Women prayed for a sudden rain that would make them pregnant and able to give birth without men. Men became idle, and found only dismissal, contempt, and derision wherever they went. Women then fell upon women, and men upon men.

2

Fuad was a man in no way different from other men. His heart almost stopped beating when he saw a beautiful woman. He told elegant Aisha he loved her. He told dark Sabah he loved her very much. He told blonde Nahla he loved her utterly. He told fair Hanan he loved her till death. And he told plump Fadwa his love was forever. Each of them had a different response, but they agreed without having met that he was not the valiant warrior who had it in him to pluck victory from decisive battle. Fuad kept away from these five women, but he realized that to win a woman he had to add a dash of polite daring to his conversation.

Staring at the bosom of fiery Maryam, he said, "I like to climb mountains." He stared at her belly and said, "And I like to go down into valleys." But with a frown on her face Maryam said in an angry voice, "I see you're an idle fellow, content only with words without climbing mountains or going down into valleys."

Fuad was now convinced women had changed. They had become warped and unfit for virile men. He married Raifa, who had dug deep into the earth for a man who would marry her, but they had not been married one week when she asked for a divorce. Her friends found that strange and pressed her to tell them the particulars, but she smiled slyly and said her husband was fond of standing in front of the mirror. She said she heard thunder and saw lightning, but no rain fell.

3

The woman and her husband were preparing to go to sleep in the darkness of night. In a soft voice, the woman said to her husband, "All the women I know love the nighttime. But I can't stand the night. Can you guess why?"

"Because at night you like to lie on your stomach," he answered without hesitation, "and I make you lie on your back."

She then lay on her stomach and said in a trembling voice, "Why don't you try to convince me of the beauties of the night, for I am a woman who doesn't hold extreme views and am willing to listen to opinions supported by arguments and proofs."

In a broken, gasping voice he spoke to her of the night. Outside cold winds were blowing, and the wife clung to her husband more closely. She said the wood in the heater had burned itself out and more was needed. He did not rush to bring wood but carried on as if the man were the wood and the woman the heater.

4

The three boys paid no heed to the burning midday sun and kept playing in the desolate alley, making enough noise for twenty. A man looked out of a window and shouted in an irate and vexed voice, "Calm down, you devils. We're trying to get some rest."

It was clear that the boys knew the man who had yelled at them, and feared him. One of them said, "Whatever you say, Abu Salim, whatever you say!"

They did not carry on with their playing but leaned against the wall and talked resentfully about school. They cursed the teacher who had failed them. The first boy said, "The Minister of Education himself is a friend of my parents, and never goes against my mother's wishes. He will go berserk when he hears what has happened, and will kick the teacher out of the school."

The second boy said, "The chief of police – he's close to my older sister and spoils me. Every time he visits, he sends me out to buy myself some cake or chocolate. I'll tell him our teacher is fat and lazy. He curses the government in front of us, and he sleeps in class and snores, and lets us do whatever we want."

The third remained silent, while his friends gazed at him in anticipation. He tried to speak, but had nothing to say. His mother did not know any men other than his father, and his sisters did not know anyone other than their husbands. He was filled with confusion, and felt he had failed a second time.

5

Hasan waited to marry until he had found an inexperienced woman, in order to be the first and last man in her life. And he married none other than the woman he was confident he had been seeking for many long years. No sooner were they alone on their first night than she swiftly helped him remove his clothes, and cried out in surprise. "The creator be praised!" she exclaimed as she gaped at him. "I used to think the little finger was on the hand and the little toe on the foot, but it seems I was wrong."

Hasan smiled with pleasure and pride, and his conviction grew that his wife was in fact the naïve and innocent woman he had been searching for.

6

Lama was accustomed to dozing off and putting in her mouth whatever happened to be in her hand. Her mother advised her in an angry and reproachful voice to get rid of her nasty habit, especially now that she was engaged and about to be married. But after marriage Lama discovered that her mother was naïve and that her advice was wrong, for what she had grown used to doing while dozing was widespread, prized, and desirable.

7

Samia did not know that her husband Mustapha could not stand her, and had married her only to please his mother. He felt that sleeping in the same bed as her was a suicide mission, and every morning a celebration for having been saved from a horrible death. She attributed his keeping away from her for several weeks to his being shy, and decided to help him get rid of his shyness. Her help began as they sat on sofas facing each other. She closed her eyes, thinking what she was doing was so seductive that no man would be able to resist. To Mustapha she appeared dead, and he almost got up to call a doctor. Samia then lazily opened her eyes and gave him looks she thought were seething with desire and would set any man on fire. But Mustapha was surprised by these glances and got ready to defend himself, thinking she was about to hit or maybe kick him.

With deliberate movements, Samia then lifted her dress and exposed her knees, expecting Mustapha to forget his shyness and come towards her crawling and pleading. She touched her flesh with drunken fingers, but to Mustapha these fingers seemed to imitate the walk of a crab or a scorpion. He asked anxiously if there were bedbugs or ants in the house, but she ignored his question, stood up, and in a loud voice complained about the extreme heat. She was about to take off her clothes when Mustapha rushed to turn on all the fans in the house, but Samia did not feel cold at all and took her clothes off anyway. Mustapha ignored her nakedness and gazed inquisitively at her clothes. Samia felt happy, then angry, and asked him what he was doing. He said he was trying to guess the price of each item of clothing, and hoped he was not wrong.

8

Fatma sat languorously in the darkened cinema watching a gripping film when a man came and took the seat next to her. In a short while he surprised her by slipping his hand under her skirt and fondling her. She was about to protest, but he leaned over and whispered in her ear that she'd better keep quiet if she didn't want to cause a scandal, one that hurt women more than it hurt men. She froze, yielding to his hand. But suddenly, she reached for him and started feeling him with nervous, greedy, and experienced fingers, trying her best to hold back the sound of her panting. His fingers became paralyzed, and he drew his hand away swiftly as if a bolt of lightning had struck it. He rose from his seat with the air of someone who suddenly remembers an important appointment and rushed out of the theater. Fatma sat back watching the absorbing film, but she now found it boring.

9

The woman was strolling in an orchard thick with trees when suddenly, out of she knew not where, a tall man appeared in front of her. He brandished a long knife and said in a coarse, threatening voice: "Careful! If you scream, I'll kill you."

The woman was filled with terror, and her face turned pale. The man was pleased to see her fear, and wanted to enjoy more of it. "Do you know what I'm going to do to you now?" he asked.

She assured him she didn't know, and had no way of knowing. He told her he was going to rape her in a way she wouldn't forget for the rest of her life. The woman sighed with relief, ignoring the knife close to her. "Are you going to rape me here, in this orchard?" she asked without fear. "Or will you take me to a house with a bed? Are you going to rape me standing up, leaning against a tree, or lying on the grass? Do you want me to take off all my clothes, or some of them, or are you going to rip them with your hands and teeth? And when you rape me, do you want me to keep quiet or moan with pain? Do you want me to cry and beg, or laugh and get excited? Are you going to rape me once, or a number of times? Will you alone rape me, or are you going to share me with your friends?"

The man found his hand stashing the knife back in his pocket, and his feet carrying him away.

10

Abdel Ghani was a bachelor who was always amazed when he saw a man in the street or the souk accompanied by an ugly wife. He would ask himself: "Are men struck by a temporary blindness and cured the moment they emerge from marriage courts shackled to wives who are like permanent blindness?"

He liked to imagine the one and only woman he would marry: tall, dark, and svelte, laughing or smiling only for him, with two big, black eyes and breasts like apples or pomegranates. She would go with him wherever he went, modestly dressed and with the same air of seriousness. Everyone who saw him would be filled with envy.

But the woman he married was not like that at all. She was short, fat and had fair skin, small eyes, and no hips. Yet no sooner did he come near her voice, her scent, and her polished, shining skin than he saw her as dark and beautiful, and exciting enough to be devoured without delay. His body felt alive and hot, and his desires raged, writhing to be released from their prison. And he did release them and, like them, he raged, finding it strange that he should be jailer and prisoner at the same time.

His wife took care every morning to accompany him to the door and say goodbye. One morning she gave him an ambiguous yet eager smile and asked him in a soft voice not to stay late at work that evening. Abdel Ghani left his place of work at noon on the pretext of suffering from a severe cold. He rushed home, only to find his wife on her hands and knees cleaning the tiles of the kitchen floor and wearing a short dress unsuitable for respectable ladies. He opened his mouth to accuse and reproach but praised her instead, suggesting she buy a shorter dress that would relieve her of the boring routine of putting on clothes and taking them off. He also offered to help her with the housework, but she refused. She reminded him she was a woman who did not care for fashion, and there was only one task for a man. She then bent over again to resume wiping the tiles with violent, rhythmic strokes.

11

I mad looked at Maha, captivated by a face like red and white roses. He suggested she come home with him to have a look at the wide, comfortable bed he had bought recently. But she smiled and proposed a picnic in the open air to celebrate her new car. He said he preferred the open air under the quilt, but she paid no attention and drove her car with sure movements, leaving behind the buildings and streets of the city. She took side roads with fields on both sides and parked her car next to a low earthen wall, "The time has come to stir your blood a little," she said to Imad.

They left the car behind and walked into the green fields, one field leading them to another, until they reached wide open ground covered with green grass and wild flowers of red, white, and yellow. "Come on," Maha shouted joyfully, "Let's race."

"What's the prize for the winner?" asked Imad immediately.

She looked at him for a moment and said with a smile, "The winner gets to do whatever he likes to the loser."

They set off running. Maha ran with the speed of a frightened gazelle chased by hunters; Imad ran with the slowness of a tortoise. The gazelle achieved a sweeping victory, but Imad readily admitted defeat, and was not ashamed. On the contrary, he lay courageously on the grass, not running away from having to pay the price, even if it was going to be heavy. But Maha nudged him with her foot and commanded him to get up. She led him without any resistance to his wide and comfortable bed. There she did all that she wanted. She placed a white butterfly on his mouth, and his searching lips tried to capture it. The tongue was not content to be a mere spectator but took an active part in the hunt, showing its skill in chasing and dodging.

12

Marwan al-Qasir was a bank employee who greatly admired Wafiqa, his colleague at work, but remained content to look at her silently and sadly. He always made sure his eyes did not show any hunger when he looked at her, for Wafiqa was not an easy woman. She was beautiful and magnetic, a serious woman, religious and resolute. She drew strict boundaries, allowing no one who spoke to her to pass beyond them. But one day Marwan mustered his courage and slipped into her hand a folded piece of paper with details of his address and an appeal to come see him any time on their day off to discuss a very urgent matter.

The moment he came home and thought about it he regretted what he had done. He accused himself of being superficial, naïve, stupid, rude, and impertinent. He was pleased the following day when Wafiqa behaved naturally, as though she had lost his letter without having read it. Yet for no particular reason he stayed home on their day off, and was surprised to see her come. He tried to speak words of welcome, but his happiness overcame all speech. He muttered something vague, which made him realize that if Wafiqa had been in a hurry to ask about the urgent matter he would have stammered and stuttered, giving the impression of being stupid and laughable.

But she did not ask any questions and followed him into a room in which there was only a sofa, a television set, and a small, low table. She sat on the sofa and said she wasn't going to stay more than a few minutes. She threw a probing look around her and said it was stifling in there as she took off her headscarf. Marwan saw what he had not seen before – long black hair and an elegant neck. These were always hidden under a secure cover that revealed only her face. His hand crept near hers and held it. Wafiqa said with pride that regardless of how hot it was her hands didn't sweat. The hand holding hers then realized there were other treasures to be had, more precious and appealing. It froze for a hesitant moment, then moved to her knee, behaving as if the knee were the head of a small child who wanted to go to sleep. Wafiqa then said she came only because she wanted to test him, to see if he really respected his colleagues and understood the nature of an innocent relationship between a man and a woman. He nodded, confident he would pass the test. He set his mouth on her fleshy lower lip, devouring it. Wafiqa said she was a decent, married woman who would rather die than cheat on her husband. She lay back on the sofa, but a cracking made it clear something had broken inside it. Laughing, Wafiqa said that whoever sold him the sofa had cheated him because it couldn't take the weight of two people. Maybe it was designed for one person only. Marwan then led her into his bedroom, where there was a bed with strong legs. He tried to remove her clothes, but she evaded his hands, her face turning red as if she had been insulted. She started to take off her clothes without any help, and threw each piece to the floor as she removed it with the gesture of someone who was never going to put it on again. Then she stood there naked, solemn, serious-looking, and self-confident, and stretched her limbs like someone ready for a long run. Marwan felt confused, but he covered her flesh with his own rather than with the quilt. She begged him not to soil the purity of her ablutions. After a few silent moments, she said in a low, panting voice: "Your name is all cheating and lying. Change it from Marwan al-Qasir (*the short*) to Marwan al-Tawil (*the long*)."

When it was dark, Wafiqa stood in front of the mirror, making sure her scarf revealed nothing other than her face. She left the house with Marwan, who stumbled along beside her, exhausted. As they walked together, heading for a bus stop nearby, Wafiqa stared in dismay at a young woman without a headscarf and said in a voice full of sadness that immoral behavior had become widespread. Marwan nodded in agreement.

13

Othman al-Maddan and Bakri al-Ghabshi were friends living in the same neighborhood and partners in a successful grocery store. From the time they were young, they never differed over anything. But Othman's wife, Naila, and Bakri's wife Ferial, disagreed from their first chance meeting at the baths when Ferial noticed that Naila was gaping pityingly at her pendulous breasts. Naila advised her to get them surgically corrected, claiming that all women were doing this in secret. It also reached Ferial that Naila was telling everyone, old and young, about what she had seen at the baths, comparing Ferial's breasts to an empty pair of socks. Now a hatred that nothing could erase sprang up between them, and they were set for a destructive battle in which no weapons would be barred. Each of them began to spread damaging and injurious rumors about the other.

One night Ferial said to Bakri, "Today the wife of your worthy partner came to see me, and accused me of marrying a man who used to be able to make love to women, while she married a man who makes love to her three times every night."

Bakri said with surprise, "What! Three times?"

Ferial laughed viciously and said, "And four on Thursday nights."

She was silent for a few moments, observing the frown on her husband's face, and said, "Do you know what she advised me to do? To divorce you. She told me her husband said a woman in my situation had the legal right to cheat on her husband and divorce him."

Bakri's face darkened, and from that moment he felt an unremitting hatred for Othman. Differences sprang up between them the following day and grew to the point of selling the store. They divided the proceeds and went their separate ways. But Bakri still wanted to take revenge on his ex-partner. He said nasty, hurtful things about him, his family, his parents, and his grandparents. Othman heard about this, but said in a forgiving voice, "There is no strength and no power save in God."

This only increased Bakri's rancor, and he decided to take his vengeance further. One day he became aware that his campaign against Othman was not being taken seriously. It needed confirmation from trustworthy and influential people. He visited Sheikh Saleh al-Mandali at his home with the pretext of giving alms for distribution to needy families. The sheikh was the imam of the neighborhood mosque. He had students, followers, and disciples, and his sayings and judgments were not disputed. He took the money from Bakri and said, as if bringing him good news, "Your reward will be with Almighty God."

Bakri said humbly, "I want nothing except His forgiveness and His mercy," and stared at the floor in silent discomfort. The sheikh asked what was wrong, and Bakri said in a trembling voice, "I'm not a man who likes to defame people, but at the same time I can't bear it when the reputation of a righteous man like yourself (May God give us more men like you!) is blackened." He then told the sheikh that his ex-partner, Othman al-Maddan, had been saying to all and sundry that he, the sheikh, led the faithful in prayer without performing his ablutions. To this the sheikh responded in a rage, "Liar, son of a liar! That happened only once. It was an absent-minded slip – and glory to Him who never slips!"

Bakri then proceeded to tell the sheikh that his ex-partner ate pig meat. The sheikh cried out in aversion and disgust, "What's this I'm hearing? A Muslim, and he eats pork?"

Bakri insisted that his ex-partner was not content with eating pork, but also made his wife do the same, until she started to like it and ask for it. The sheikh's disgust mounted. Though the two were alone in the room, Bakri looked around cautiously and whispered in an agitated voice. "He also says something which I can't believe and which I'm even ashamed to mention. He says you practice the secret habit."

The sheikh said, "A liar! A thousand times a liar! And how could I possibly be doing that when my wife has been more like a sister for two years, three months, and five days?"

Bakri took hold of the sheikh's hand in a gesture of encouragement and said, "Where is the earth from the stars? You, dear sir, are older and grander than him. Pay no heed to what he says, for he is a worthless fellow who doesn't have the legal authority to declare what's lawful and what's not. He's not satisfied to have his wife and her mother but chases after boys, as I discovered by mere chance. I became worried about my reputation, and ended my partnership with him at a loss."

The wrinkles on the sheikh's face became deeper as he said in an angry, shaking voice, "God save us from the

---

Zakaria Tamer

cursed Devil! God save us from the cursed Devil! It is true that the Devil has followers who live to spread evil on this earth."

A few days later, Sheikh Saleh was leaning on his cane and winding his way through the alley that led to his house, when Abul 'Ala, the toughest man in the neighborhood, blocked his path and kissed his hand with reverence and humility. He begged the sheikh to pray for him, that God might guide his path away from a life of mischief. But the sheikh said abruptly, "How can I pray to God for you when my heart is full of worry, sorrow, and anger? Prayer will not be answered unless it comes from a pure heart."

Abul 'Ala then said. "Death to anyone who has angered our revered sheikh! Tell me his name, then go recite the opening chapter of the Qur'an for his soul."

Sheikh Saleh then leaned against the wall of a house, as if to prevent himself from falling, and said with sadness and bitterness in his voice, "Son, God is my witness. All my life I've taken care to love everyone, rich and poor. But the deeds of Othman al-Maddan are contrary to the laws of God and his Prophet, and they have infuriated me, making me hate that dissolute, immoral, debauched and godless man."

Abul 'Ala was stunned to hear this and said: "But what I know of him is that he is a man who prays, fasts, and pays his share of alms, and has been on the hajj twice."

Sheikh Saleh laughed in derision and said, "It seems, my son, that you've forgotten the Devil was once an angel himself."

Sheikh Saleh then sighed with sadness and said, "It is the duty of every Muslim to fight godlessness. Every believer who rids the world of a godless man will enter Paradise without being held to account."

30

Abul 'Ala again kissed the sheikh's hand and said in a soft, trembling voice, "God permitting, all of us will go to paradise."

It was only a few days later that the body of Othman al-Maddan was found stabbed to death. Those who last saw him alive said he had performed the evening prayer at the neighborhood mosque standing right behind Sheikh Saleh al-Mandali and had left for his house nearby. He never reached it. His wife Naila cried until her eyes were swollen. She wore clothes of mourning, and swore she would never take them off as long as she was alive. Bakri's wife, Ferial, spread the rumor that Naila was in mourning over her cat, which had been run over by a car.

14

Hamid was sleeping when all of a sudden the roof collapsed on top of him. He awoke with a feeling of terror, and related what he saw to an aged neighbor known for his ability to interpret dreams.

"Do you want a lie that will make you happy," asked the neighbor, "or a truth that will hurt and make you feel sad?"

"Let me hear the lie first," Hamid answered.

"You'll be saved from cares that you think are mountains but which turn out to be nothing but dust," said the neighbor.

"Now, I'll hear the truth," Hamid said.

The neighbor smiled. He advised Hamid to keep his eyes open day and night, observing his wife's behavior.

"But, as you know, I'm not married," Hamid said in utter surprise.

"You'll marry soon," said the neighbor, "and don't forget to keep watch over the woman you marry, or you'll regret it."

The neighbor's prophecy came true. In a few months Hamid married a widow with much experience. He did not neglect his neighbor's advice, and kept watch over his wife like one who expected something bad to happen. But he forgot to watch himself, with the result that his wife caught him in the guest room in very close contact with his youthful guest. She immediately threw the guest out of the house. Hamid spoke to his wife in a broken voice about his respect for ancient customs that called upon people to practice generosity with guests, but she cut him off angrily. "Can't I also be a guest to practice your generosity on? Why didn't you let me know what you preferred and what I also prefer?"

And she bent forward, just like the youthful guest, and Hamid admitted he had been blind and ignorant.

15

The birds whet their beaks when they see Naziha, and say she's a little fig tree whose fruit is ripe and ready to eat. Yet no one has reached for her, even though all around her were men with a deep, savage, and ancient hunger which must one day get all it wants. One evening Naziha found herself on the telephone to her mother, sobbing and gasping. Her mother was surprised and asked, "Are you crying because you regret having left your family home and rented a place of your own where you live by yourself as good-for-nothing people do?"

Naziha reproached her mother for her question and said she was crying because she came back home from work tired as usual and was surprised to find a man she had never seen before in her kitchen. She didn't know how he got into the house, but he demanded that she marry him right away. Her mother said, interrupting, "An offer like this is not to be rejected if the man is rich and comes from a respectable family."

Naziha made it clear to her mother that she had turned down his proposal and had advised him to see a psychiatrist, but he had offered to marry her right away, without a

35

wedding. The mother asked inquisitively. "And what did you do?"

Naziha said in an irate voice. "Don't ask what I did; ask what he did. He carried me like a baby and set me down on the kitchen table. Then he married me without a wedding."

The mother asked, puzzled, "I don't understand. How could he marry you without a wedding?"

Naziha answered: "What took place can't be spoken about, and don't forget I'm very modest."

The mother then asked in a cheerful voice, "Did you resist?"

Naziha answered, "I resisted with the strength of a hundred women. There isn't a spot on his body that I didn't bite with my teeth or scratch with my fingers."

The mother chuckled, as if all she had heard was nothing but a joke. Then she asked, "Are you sure that what happened to you isn't one of your usual fantasies?"

Naziha did not get the chance to answer because the line suddenly went dead. She waited for her mother to call back, but the telephone never rang. Naziha was angry with her mother and thought her egotistical. She then called Hanan, whom she considered the best of all her friends, and asked her to listen to what she had to say without a single word of interruption. She related to her that as she was about to open the door of her house she was taken by surprise by a young man and woman who pushed her inside, put a gag around her mouth, and tied her hands and feet. They then disappeared into the bedroom for an hour or two and came out laughing, their cheeks rosy. They thanked her as they left the house, the girl saying in a whisper as she untied her, "You're a woman and you know the problems young men and women face when they don't have a place."

"I've said all there was to say," Naziha said to Hanan. "Now it's your turn to speak. Tell me what you think of what happened."

"Next time," Hanan said, "remember you're the mistress of the house. Let them do what they want on condition they tie you up inside the bedroom."

Naziha let out an indignant cry and hung up. She then called the police and told them in a halting, trembling, and alarmed voice that a strange man whom she didn't know had forced his way into her house and intended to rob her of her clothes, jewelry, and furniture. She said he was going to take even the clothes on her back and rape her at least twice if they didn't rush to her rescue. The policeman to whom she was talking asked, "This man, where is he now?"

"He grumbled about feeling dirty and went into the bathroom to take a bath," Naziha said. "And he's now singing in a loud voice that disturbs the neighbors."

The policeman said, advising, "Try to run away at the first opportunity that presents itself."

"This house is my house," Naziha cried out in an astonished, disapproving, and distressed voice. "So why should I be the one to run away?"

"What does he look like?" asked the policeman, whispering. "Remember the details. Details are important to us."

If I remember correctly," answered Naziha, "he is tall and well-built, with blond hair and a smile that starts in his eyes and then drops down to his lips."

"We'll be sending a police patrol as soon as possible," the policeman said. "Keep calm and try not to make him angry or provoke him. Do whatever he asks, so that no harm will come to you."

Naziha's fingers let go of the receiver, and she listened, but no sound of a man singing in the bath reached her ears. She smiled in confusion, for when the police arrived they would find that the stranger was content just to bathe and run away.

16

Abu Said al-Deeb was smoking his narghile and contemplating the slowly setting sun as he sat on the balcony of his third-floor apartment that looked over the gardens of the other buildings. He was eating fruit that his wife had peeled, cut, and offered to him. There was a sudden knock on the door, and someone came in to let him know his youngest son had been arrested while taking part in a demonstration that called for a change in the government. Abu Said became angry and shouted at his wife, "Did you hear that, Lady Amina? Your son is in prison. And why? Because he's against the government. Do you see the fruits of the way you brought him up?"

"Your children are just like you," answered Amina. "None of them ever listens to advice, and they do exactly as they please."

Abu Said said with a sad and disapproving voice, "This happens to me! My son arrested in a demonstration against the government! What have we to do with the government? We don't know it, and it doesn't know us. It's not our neighbor, and we're not its neighbor."

Abu Said remembered with sadness his grandfather, who got into a fight when he was quite an old man, stabbed five of the most famous bullies with his dagger, and came out unscathed. He remembered his father, who had spent his life one month at home and one year in prison and never stopped smuggling and selling contraband guns. He also remembered Garbage Dump Neighborhood, where he was born and grew up. He remembered its people, who were angry because of the name and had changed it to Highest Honor Neighborhood. But the new name did not stop other neighborhoods from mocking its inhabitants. He felt compelled to leave it and, to silence his mockers, had lived in one of the modern houses scattered about on streets that were not narrow alleys. And when he remembered his sons, whom people held in awe, and who fought with their own shadows and spread fear everywhere, his resentment against his youngest son grew. "This is not my son," he said to his wife, "and I disown him from now till the Day of Judgment."

But before long there was another knock on the door. Someone came in who corrected the previous news. The youngest son had not been arrested in a demonstration but had been dragged away naked from the room of a prostitute when during the night the police had raided houses of ill repute. Abu Said then sighed with relief and asked about the prostitute. Was she beautiful or ugly? Did she deserve her payment, or was his son hoodwinked? He was told the prostitute spoiled his son by offering her services free. Abu Said's eyes almost filled with tears of pride in a family that could still go from one glorious deed to another.

17

The most beautiful women jostled each other to work for Muhsin al-Muhsin. He was famous for this: if he promised someone a beautiful woman, he would be exposed in a few hours because the woman would turn out to be not merely beautiful but also enchanting, obedient, and modest in her needs.

Rich and well-known families, as well as poor and little-known ones, competed in welcoming him into their homes. He gratefully accepted their invitations and found in every home something that excited and entertained him, and helped support and sustain his work with new and enthusiastic recruits.

Muhsin al-Muhsin was a truly attractive man. Many women loved him, and he loved many women. Then suddenly he became fed up with women; he turned a cold eye on them and fought against a disgust that he tried to hide. He fell in love with a wall in the souk and welcomed the thought of himself turning into a wall of black stone, facing the wall that he loved. He was rewarded with days of contentment and happiness, to the extent that he did not mind children urinating on him. As for the women who used to work for him, they became ugly and rude, and prey to limitless greed, promising a lot but giving little. Men used to come to him to complain. They tried to convince him to come back and help them, but he held tenaciously to his silence, feeling pleased he was a wall. His happiness did not last long, however, for an official order to widen the street as quickly as possible was promulgated. Many walls were brought down, and one of them hoped its stones would be used again in building a prison for women.

18

Suheir Salmoon was a woman beyond compare. She became famous for never having turned down a solicitation from any man because, she said, she had enough tender and desirable flesh to satisfy those hungry for it, regardless of how many there were. She gave her gifts without asking for payment, saying in a trembling voice she had no money to give alms to the poor, the wretched, and the orphans.

One night her house and bedroom were full of male guests, and they all agreed her fair flesh was a burning snow that did not turn into water and that her lips were more beautiful than wild berries growing in any forest. The praise embarrassed her and she murmured, her face reddening, "True beauty consists in moral conduct."

Her guests then praised her firm and supple morals, their warmth and rightness, and the redness in her face grew more intense until she seemed like a drunken woman. She then wet her lips with her tongue and informed her guests that, on that very day, she had accidentally touched a wall made of stone, and green grass had covered it instantly. The men rushed to be blessed by her hand, but one of them objected, saying he didn't believe her words because no sooner did her hand touch flesh than it went wild, lost its flexibility and became stiff and hard like a stone. The guests laughed as they had never laughed before.

Suheir was surprised when a young man whom she knew to be shy like a girl cried out, "Whether it is to be honor or disgrace, the proof of the pudding is in the eating."

Then, bowing politely in front of her, he asked her to touch anything that pleased her and if green grass grew on it then she would be telling the truth. Suheir was stunned, but hid her hurt feelings, for she was telling nothing less than the truth. That night she slept in extreme misery, and a strange visitor came to her in a dream. His upper part was in deep darkness and the lower suffused with a blinding light. The visitor said to her that her reward for a life full of pious and generous deeds was that upon waking she would find herself able to fly. She woke up immediately and found she could indeed fly like a small, fast airplane. She flew away and disappeared from sight. The men waited anxiously and impatiently, but she never came back. They did not believe she would desert them, and said her prolonged absence was because she had lost her way in the wide-open sky or had flown over forbidden territory.

19

Huda took care to wake up early and step quickly out of the house, leaving her husband sleeping the sleep of the dead. She walked through streets that were nearly empty, heading for a famous bakery. She bought fresh, hot bread, which her husband liked more than meat or fruit and would be very pleased to have for breakfast. Suddenly people started running as fast as they could in the direction of the main square. Curiosity got the better of Huda, and she followed without thinking. Once there, she saw a gallows already in place, soldiers carrying guns, a man about to be hanged, and a sun about to rise. The noose was already around the condemned man's neck, and he cast a glance upon the spectators milling around the scaffold. He heard only the sounds they made but saw no one except Huda, the woman with dark hair and fair hands and face, staring at him with eyes as wide open as they could be. She noticed that he had seen her, and she smiled like a child on whom snow had fallen for the first time.

When the condemned man became aware that what he was standing on was about to slip away from under his feet, he gave Huda a look that appealed for help. She was amazed, for she had never thought that one day a thin young man with a gentle face and gentle eyes would seek her help. For a few fleeting moments she felt he was her younger brother hanging on to the edge of her dress asking for protection but she did not know what to do. The hubbub and the crowd around the gallows grew more dense, especially when the young man dangled, a lifeless corpse with a blue face. Huda felt she was about to suffocate and walked quickly away, leaving the people behind and heading home before the bread got cold. She came into the bedroom and found her husband awake. "Now that you're awake," she said, "I'll make your breakfast."

"The world won't go to pieces," he said as he reached for her, "if breakfast is delayed."

He started pulling at her clothes. She was disgusted and felt like moving away from his hands, but she did not stir. She smiled, pretending she could not wait for what was coming next, and her hands began to help his. She was stunned by what she was doing and became angry at herself for being so weak. She longed to cry out at the top of her voice, but she jumped into the bed with a cheerful motion and slipped under the quilt as she said, "A little while ago, I saw a man being hanged."

"Many are hanged every day," he said, laughing, "without rope or spectators."

She said nothing. "What did he do to deserve hanging?" he asked. "Disobey the traffic laws?"

"I heard the policemen and other people say he killed an entire family because one of them had killed his brother," Huda answered. "He killed the men and the women, and the boys and the girls. He even killed their cat, and felt sorry for no one except the cat."

"This is the state of the world," he said as he embraced her. "He who kills only ten people is a criminal to be hanged. But he who kills hundreds of thousands is a hero among heroes."

In that silent room with the door bolted and the curtains drawn Huda saw with half-closed eyes a man moving on top of a woman who had around her neck a rope that forced her to gasp for breath, and he was ready to choke her every time she tried to break free of him.

The man gave the woman a long, hard look, like a merchant who had bought a cow and wanted to make sure he had not been cheated. She felt embarrassed and closed her eyes and wanted to turn into lifeless flesh, but her body paid no heed and set to doing all that pleased it and made her angry. She heard her husband say jokingly that after all this effort she would certainly give birth in nine months. She was about to say something disapproving, as she might to one who would never one day father any child she would bring into the world, but she chose to say nothing. She imagined that she had gone back to the gallows at night and cut the noose surrounding the neck of the hanged man, and that he had felt his neck with his fingers and with a distracted look had thanked her in a halting voice and promised he would never kill another cat. At that moment her husband stretched and yawned and asked about breakfast. She wanted to tell him to hurry out to the nearest restaurant, but she quickly put on some clothes and rushed into the kitchen.

20

Munir admired Munira and her name before their marriage, but he did not love her then. He loved her after marriage without ever telling her about his feelings. He loved her laugh and the look in her eyes when she was excited, and loved her shy but daring manner. They lived together for three years that were free of crises. One morning he was surprised by her sudden death – she who was never sick and who had gotten him used to waking up every morning to the aroma of the coffee she prepared for him while he was still in bed. But on that day he woke up late and found Munira lying next to him in very deep sleep. He tried to wake her but she did not wake up. The doctor determined she had died at dawn from a heart attack. Munir did not cry as she was laid in her coffin and taken out of the house. And he did not cry as he walked down the alleyways behind those carrying the coffin on their shoulders. He did not cry as she was laid to rest under the ground. His people and her people blamed him, accusing him of ingratitude and forgetfulness of sharing bread and salt. Munir did not try to defend himself and slept alone in the bed where he used to sleep with his wife. Munira came to him in a dream and said he shouldn't feel sad because she wouldn't part from him and wouldn't let him feel in need of anyone. She visited him another night and advised him to end his relationship with one of his friends, but he said in utter surprise, "But he's a brother, and not just a friend."

She insisted that his friend was a drug dealer in secret and would soon be arrested and sent to prison for twenty or thirty years and would expose all his friends to serious difficulties. Munir quickly found an excuse to pick a fight that led to enmity and an end to the relationship with his friend. No more than a few weeks had passed when his friend was chosen as minister of the interior, and he set about serving his own interests and the interests of his friends. Munir then became resentful of Munira and her advice. When he decided to invest in a house, Munira advised him not to buy because house prices were going to fall in a few weeks. Munir changed his mind about buying, but house prices quickly went up, and his resentment of Munira and her tips increased. She then visited him in his dream with her face in a frown and asked him not to listen to his family's insistent demands to marry the woman they had chosen for him. Munira said this woman would drive anyone who married her crazy. He did not listen to her and married the woman, and he did not become crazy. He mocked Munira, and she became angry and stopped visiting him. He then married a second woman and a third and a fourth. To friends who found this strange, he said, "He who marries four will have a life of ease because they will compete in pampering him and making his life comfortable. They will differ among themselves, and this will double their efforts to win his favor."

What he said was true, for he could see his four wives arguing among themselves and hating each other. He was pleased with the success of his plan, not realizing that their argument was nothing more than an act put on to please him once it became clear to them that they had an excellent life, with nothing to spoil it except his existence. They would be in heaven if he were to disappear. They competed in cooking fatty foods for him and desserts that relied heavily on unadulterated cream and pure ghee. Munir ate voraciously, as if each meal was going to be his last, and his wives competed in seducing him day and night, not leaving him alone until he turned into a thing suitable for throwing into the garbage. He changed, became fat, and was struck by all the known diseases, all of which led to his leaving the house in a coffin with a bearded man in front who cried out: "O you who hear this! Forgive the deceased Munir Ibn Said Ibn Khadija."

After his death his wives did not part, but lived together in the house. Munir had left them in need of no one. All four of them took care to visit his grave every week wearing black clothes, but Munir would get angry, believing that their visits had no other purpose than to make sure he was still dead.

21

Summer was hot in the alley. The noon sun forced those who lived there to disappear into their cool houses. The alley became empty, as if a secret curfew had been declared. But Laila, who was ten years old and wearing a short blue dress, remained in the alley near the door of her home leaning her back against the wall. On his way back to his house, her father saw an old man with unruly hair clinging to his daughter. He drew the knife he had been using to slaughter and cut up sheep in his shop and came at him, raging. The old man lost no time saying in a panting voice that he was lost and was merely asking the way. He was forced to come close to her so that she could hear his faint voice. The father paid no heed, and advanced toward the old man, but Laila cried out in a frightened voice, warning him not to come any closer because the old man was hiding a snake that stirred under his clothes. The father went into a rage and fell upon the old man. His raised knife was trembling, overcome with a mixture of joy, excitement, and alarm, and looking forward to something new, unfamiliar, and different from the necks of lambs and chickens. It plunged headlong in the direction of the old man, and its sharp, wide blade sank into flesh and blood. The knife found it strange that its owner did not cry out "God is great!" as usual.

The men of the alley worked together without talking or making any kind of sound. They put the corpse and the head in a sack made of sturdy cloth and carried it to the shop of the father, who ground the flesh, pulverized the bones, and made sausages that he fed to the many stray dogs and cats. The women worked together, washing the alley with soap and hot water. They washed it so well that the people who lived there took pride for a long time in its cleanliness and its plump cats and dogs.

22

The marriage of Abdel Sattar and Laila was a clamorous event in which everyone in the neighborhood took part, but he was not destined to complete his honeymoon. Three days into it he was put under temporary arrest, and when he was released ten years later everyone in the neighborhood – men, women, and children – were there waiting for him. No sooner did they catch a glimpse of him coming through the gate than the women broke into trills of joy, the boys raised a din, and the men rushed to embrace him warmly and congratulate him with words coming straight from the heart. He thanked them all in a trembling voice that could barely be heard for the clamor. But all this din ceased when he scanned the crowd for his wife and saw her standing there, surrounded by five children of different ages, shapes and sizes – fat, thin, short, tall, with fair and dark complexions, and with blond and black hair. Laila saw him looking at her and waved with one hand while the other wiped away the tears. He approached her, his heart beating wildly and, with both hands reached out to the small, soft hand that was wiping away the tears and took it as if it were held out to rescue someone about to drown.

Abdel Sattar stared at Laila in amazement, for she had grown more beautiful and youthful, and looked much younger than her age. The neighborhood folk shouted back and forth in make-believe disapproval, but Abdel Sattar laughed and said, "Legally she's my wife. Have you forgotten that I married her according to the laws of God and His Prophet?"

The noise got louder as it mingled with laughter, and they walked with him to his house. Once there he sat in the shade of the bitter orange tree in the courtyard and sipped his coffee slowly. Suddenly he pointed with his index finger to the five children who were standing apart from him, some eyeing him with hostility and others with shy looks, and said, "Who are these children? Are they the children of neighbors, or relatives?"

His wife immediately started praising the neighborhood for its manliness and gallantry because it had fulfilled its obligation and provided well for a woman who had lost her family and was living alone. Abdel Sattar interrupted, asking her about the children again. She gave him a look of amazement and surprise. "What a question!" she said. "Poor man! Don't you recognize your children? It's true that prison weakens the memory." Abdel Sattar said in a questioning voice, "Were you pregnant when I was arrested?"

"No," Laila answered. "I wasn't pregnant. What a shame! As you remember, the honeymoon lasted only three days, and we were bashful."

Then Laila sighed and said, "But there's no other place like our neighborhood. Do you know Mr. Said, the elementary school teacher? He was the one who volunteered to help me with the first child. Men like him are rare. I can't describe to you the trouble he went to."

"And the second son?" Abdel Sattar asked.

"Look at him closely," Laila answered, "and you can tell right away who helped me with him. There's only one man in our neighborhood with blond hair, Abdel Hafez, the notable. He helped me even though he is married to two insatiable women."

"And the third?" asked Abdel Sattar.

"You know the man who helped me with this one," Laila answered, "and you will approve of my choice: morality, piety, fasting, pilgrimage, and prayer every time the call to prayer is made. Perhaps our son will inherit some of these virtues."

"And the fourth?" asked Abdel Sattar.

"I'm fairly sure the help came from the doctor," Laila answered. "I remember he used to make sure that all drugs for me and the children were free."

"And the fifth?" asked Abdel Sattar.

"You and I don't like a liar," Laila answered. "I'm at a loss to know who was the father in this case due to all the help I got from ten young men or more, each of them taller than a palm tree and wider than a door." Abdel Sattar's fingers let go of the coffee cup, which fell to the ground and shattered, and he squatted against a wall made of rough black stone. He wanted to cry, as he had cried when beaten severely in prison, but his eyes remained dry.

23

Salem smelled the fragrance of her hair, and said it was sweeter than the smell of grass. But Muna laughed a strange laugh and said grass was preferred by sheep, goats, and cows. She lured him into sleep, saying that keeping his eyes wide open day and night in order to watch her was harmful and confusing. He could not resist her charm, and slept on her knee as a child sleeps on its mother's knees. Muna did not leave him alone but followed deep into his sleep. She stood on the balcony of a palace and looked down over thousands of men. "Today," she spoke to them in a voice like water, "you will get some of what you've been wanting but haven't had the courage to ask for openly."

She then started to undress in a manner that made each of them feel she was undressing only for him. "Aren't you ashamed of what you're doing?" Salem asked her reproachfully.

Muna laughed and said she wasn't doing anything other than turning the faces of these men with the proud mustaches a little red. Salem's face reddened in anger, and he found it strange to feel hungry while still asleep. "What did you cook today?" he asked.

"Serving the masses comes first," answered Muna, "then serving the husband."

At that moment, a small bird landed on Muna's palm and searched for the seeds it used to pick with its beak, but her fingers grabbed it in a sudden movement and closed on its neck, not letting go until it had choked to death. Salem woke up terrified, only to find Muna sleeping next to him, a cross between a desirable woman and a gentle child.

24

The village of Dhaghbit had snow-covered mountains summer and winter, fields full of fruitful trees, pure, refreshing air, and springs – too many to count. People came from nearby towns and villages for rest and recreation, but the women of the village wished Dhaghbit would vanish from the earth so that they could be rid of their boorish men, for in their village a woman could not even mutter "good morning" to her husband unless he gave her permission.

But something happened in Dhaghbit that people could not recount because it would have been too offensive to speak of it. Many homes were broken into late at night by a strange man who, it was said, wanted to rob and rape, but the householders did not complain to the police at the station which was always filled with people yawning. No news about the thief's success or failure was allowed to escape. It was observed, however, that the women of Dhaghbit started to ignore their husbands' orders and did exactly as they pleased.

There lived in Dhaghbit an old man who until his retirement did not know any other profession than soldiering. He lived alone in a big house that had many entrances and was difficult to guard. It occurred to him that the thief might want to raid his home. If there was no one there worthy of being raped, there was certainly something worth being stolen. He started keeping watch at night, staying awake with his gun, waiting for the thief. He did not have to wait long, for without knowing how it happened he found himself face to face with the man, holding the gun to his neck and ordering him not to move. The thief obeyed without complaining, and the old man removed a dagger and a revolver from him and tied him up with the thick ropes he had readied for the occasion. He sat in front of him smoking a cigarette, and asked him what he had done in Dhaghbit, and the thief answered immediately and with enthusiasm. It turned out that what he was saying was different from what was commonly believed. He claimed with pride that in every house he entered he raped the man in front of his wife. He said to the old man, "Ask any woman about me, and she will tell you that I treated her with respect, the way I treat my sister and my grandmother."

The thief added proudly that there were very few men left in Dhaghbit whom he hadn't raped, and nothing was going to save them.

He then laughed and said to the old man, "Don't let big mustaches and big talk impress you. Many of the men weren't ashamed before their wives and asked me to rape them a second time."

The old man was in a quandary. If he handed the thief to the police and they were to take down his testimony, a huge scandal would erupt that might scorch everything in sight. And it was not reasonable to keep him a prisoner in the house forever. The old man then rushed to ask the men whom the thief claimed he had raped to come over, and sought their advice. They spoke not a word but drew their knives and descended upon the old man and the thief. They tore them to pieces, and their corpses disappeared.

When only a few weeks had passed, the women of Dhaghbit went back to listening to their husbands' orders with a shudder, rushed to obey them, and wished that Dhaghbit would vanish under the snows.

25

Bahiya was a beautiful woman surrounded by meddlesome neighbors whose eyes watched her day and night. They repeated stories about her and her four children by unknown fathers that were so scandalous they could turn a coal-black bull white – stories that drove a bearded neighbor rashly to suggest that Bahiya should be stoned to death. His suggestion was not followed because their streets had no stones, and to bring them from where they could be found needed time, effort, and money. Bahiya heard all that was said about her and received it calmly, quietly, and with self-possession, contenting herself with cheerful, protective smiles and taking care to keep anger at a distance. She never tried to defend herself by speaking of her legal but secret marriages that sometimes stretched the limits of credibility. Her first husband was a jinni with irresistible charm, and he was not a believer. He loved her at first sight, but she refused to marry him because he was not a Muslim. The jinni suffered the despair of the loser and begged her to tell him something about Islam. Her words were so warm and effective that his heart trembled with humility, and he immediately declared he was a Muslim, having sincerely borne witness that there was no god but God and that Muhammad was his prophet.

He married her and became the father of her first son. Their marriage ended tragically when the husband took part in a failed military coup and was arrested and executed without trial. Bahiya mourned and took to wearing black, when the second jinni to become her husband noticed her. He admired her in her mourning clothes and asked for something not appropriate for a decent woman to give, and she became angry. She acted like one possessed by the jinn and rejected him in the harshest possible way. But the jinni became even more infatuated, for she appeared more beautiful when angry. He waited years before she agreed to marry him, and he fathered her second and third sons. He could not become the father of her fourth because an out-of-control car driven by a drunken soldier hit him, turning him into pieces of torn flesh and shattered bones.

Bahiya married a third jinni, whom she loved, but she bore him no children because she hated his poverty, his laziness, and the odor of his breath. She sang with joy when he divorced her.

She then married a fourth out of greed for what he owned, and he became the father of her fourth son. But she discovered that his huge wealth had come from embezzlement and bribery and wasted no time in divorcing him because she hated ill-gotten gains and her hands refused to touch them without a pair of thick gloves.

What happened to Bahiya convinced her she had no luck in husbands – there being no bench for her in the garden of lovers – and she decided not to marry again. She turned down the most desirable suitors, both human and jinn, and devoted her life entirely to raising her four sons until they became respectable men with money and influence and standing in the community. Bahiya's neighbors then woke up to the fact that she was a fine woman worthy of respect, and rushed to endear themselves to her. Women came asking for advice when there was a crisis that had no resolution. Bahiya did not change even after death. Whenever a woman came to her grave to complain about her husband's boorishness and stupidity, she would be surprised to discover when she went home that he had changed, having now become finer than a summer cloud, obeying with pleasure any order he was given.

26

The funeral procession passing through the streets was that of Akram al-Aqrash, who died without having married, and with no relatives to inherit the immense fortune he left behind. He did not leave a will. The women mourners walking behind the coffin were more distressed than the men. Their tears flowed freely, and they wailed and lamented, tearing their clothes and walking with heads shamelessly uncovered. When the procession arrived at the cemetery, the women fell into a fight. Each claimed the dead man had not married her only because she was already married but that he was the real father of all her boys and girls. Very quickly, however, the grieving women resorted less and less to words and more and more to slapping, punching, and kicking. A number of them cut down thick branches from the trees in the cemetery and used them as sticks, which descended with painful blows upon the heads and backs of the other women. Some of the women gathered stones that hit back without mercy at those wielding the clubs. Soon the graveyard was strewn with women's bodies stained with blood. A man with a white beard, exclaiming there was no power and no strength save in God, edged himself into the fray in an effort to calm things down. He was surprised by a blow to the forehead from a hefty stick that made him reel and fall to the ground, moaning like a pregnant woman whose time had come. The stones falling all around forced him to muster his energies and crawl toward the open grave in order to hide. The gravedigger was dumbfounded and could not believe his eyes. He rushed out of the cemetery in the hope of finding a policeman, a doctor, or an ambulance. As for the husbands of the feuding women, they were content to stare at the coffin on the ground, angry at the one who had cheated them by pretending he was an old man who couldn't take a step without leaning on a stick. They kicked the coffin with malicious joy. Akram al-Aqrash cried out from his prone position inside the coffin, asking to be buried quickly, but his cry was lost in the uproar of the fighting women and no one heard it.

27

Bashir tried to scream for his wife, but the cries that came from his slack lips were like a feeble rattling in the throat. The room, its air depleted, shrank, and he collapsed. At that moment his wife walked in and was surprised to find him lying on the floor. "What's all this laziness?" she asked in a loud, disapproving voice. "If you want to rest, go lie down on the bed."

But she heard no reply, and went on, "I forgot that you're annoyed when I speak. And you have the right to feel that way because you're not the one who washes your clothes and irons them."

She took off her dress with a sudden movement and stood in front of the wardrobe mirror looking at her body with pleasure and admiration. "Look!" She said to Bashir. "See how the exercises you always ridiculed have given me a waist more beautiful than that of a young girl's."

She stretched, looking at Bashir expectantly, then muttered in complaint, "Drowsy at night and tired during the day!"

She then put on a blue dress, and said to Bashir, "What do you think of this dress? Don't you agree that the blue agrees with my fair complexion and black hair?"

She received no answer, and said mockingly, "I'm sorry. I forgot you can't stand to see me elegantly dressed, but would rather see me go out of the house in clothes that aren't even fit for beggars."

She heard no comment form him and said as she walked to the door, "If my mother calls and asks about me, tell her I'll be there in one hour."

No reply reached her ears, and she left the house feeling frustrated and angry.

28

Khadija al-Mahhar left no one she knew without swearing to them that as long as she had even one breath left her son Ismail would never marry Nawal al-Rata. It wasn't becoming for someone like her son to marry someone without brilliant family connections, one who moreover was kind to everyone and who charmed young people and corrupted them. Nawal's mother was a half-wit, and her father was hired out to a carpenter. Khadija believed that her son hated what she hated, liked what she liked, and would not go against her wishes. She did not believe it when he left the home in which he was indulged and honored and provided with every comfort, and married Nawal and lived with her in a house smaller than a tin of sardines. Khadija put on the darkest clothes in her wardrobe and asked all her acquaintances to commiserate with her for the loss of her son, whom death had snatched away while still in the prime of youth. What she said turned out to be a forewarning of what actually happened, for Ismail did not finish his honeymoon. He was hit by a drunken driver, and his mother never had a chance to see him again except as a lifeless corpse who could not respond to her scolding and reproach. And there, in a bleak corridor in the hospital, the mother came face to face with the weeping Nawal, and she glowered at her with harsh and threatening looks. But she was surprised to discover that the tears flowing from Nawal's eyes were genuine tears that came from a wounded heart which could not be healed. Nawal appeared to her at that moment to be a small, weak creature that kept shaking and couldn't stand firmly on its feet; she was like someone about to die but was condemned to suffer without finding release in death. She rushed toward her and embraced her as though she were embracing Ismail, and allowed her to cry herself out on her breast. She swore that Nawal must come home with her after the funeral and sleep in Ismail's bed, which Nawal had never seen before. That night was followed by others, and Nawal lived with her mother-in-law, who never stopped exclaiming in a voice full of piety, "How generous is the Lord! With one hand He takes away, and with the other He provides."

Nothing annoyed Nawal in her new life save her mother-in-law's insistence that she marry again. The mother described the character of those whom she had picked out for Nawal, and at the end of the evening would ask her to talk about Ismail. She listened in amazement, as if she had known nothing about him.

29

Rida Jalal had became famous among the inhabitants of al-Ma'mun Street for being a strange man with brothers among the jinn who rushed to his aid when he fell on hard times. His house played a role in spreading his fame. The houses on al-Ma'mun Street consisted of entire floors in tall, modern buildings made of stone and cement, while Rida's was an old house made of mud and straw. Many found it strange that the officials responsible for city planning turned a blind eye to this house and did not order its demolition, removal, and replacement by a modern building. They found no satisfactory explanation, except that the house had an invisible master who protected it and made sure it remained standing in its present state.

Rida Jalal had inherited the house from his parents after they died, and lived in it by himself even though it had many rooms. However, at night the house changed. It was transformed into a blaze of light, with the sounds of laughing men and women and playing children coming from it. Passersby on al-Ma'mun Street invoked the name of the Compassionate and Merciful God and ran into their houses, feeling happy they were still standing and had not disappeared.

None of the inhabitants of al-Ma'mun Street could claim they'd ever caught a glimpse of Rida buying fruit. Some accused him of being exceedingly miserly, while others spread the rumor that his jinn brothers brought him the most delicious fruits every night. Men avoided his company, except for Safwan al-Mughrabi, who denied the existence of the jinn and was not afraid of them. One day he took it upon himself to heckle Rida. He gave him a punch so powerful it threw Rida to the ground, and said, "This blow is not for you but for your jinn brothers."

Rida rose dizzily from the ground, and some men came between them, making sure the fray did not continue. But no sooner did night come than the police burst into the house of Safwan al-Mughrabi, searched it, and found a large quantity of narcotics. They arrested Safwan and took him to the station, where they set upon him with continuous blows that knew no mercy, with the intention of forcing him to admit where he had gotten hold of the drugs. But he refused to confess and died under torture. Afterwards, it was rumored in al-Ma'mun Street that the last policeman to give Safwan the fatal kick on the head had said, "This kick is not from me, but from my brother Rida."

Rida was a bachelor, and it was rumored in al-Ma'mun Street that he had not yet married because he had a jinn wife who had given him a son and a daughter, and they too belonged to the race of the jinn like their mother and not the race of men like their father. But Rida surprised everyone by marrying Jamila al-Halim. The men said, "And why should we find this strange? Rida is a Muslim, and he has the right to marry four women, not just two."

Jamila al-Halim happened to be a woman who had had many husbands. Every time she married a man, she divorced him within a week or two in disgust, ridiculing his lack of manliness. Many felt sorry for Rida and expected he would get the same treatment as those who were his betters. But Jamila changed and became more like an obedient slave. If Rida ordered her to die she would have done so, and if he ordered her to live she would go on living.

Jamila did not hide the secret of her transformation from the women of her neighborhood. She told them her husband lay on top of her as soon as he had finished his evening prayer, and would not leave her until the muezzin had called the dawn prayers. He would then leave her and rush to the mosque, to gain double reward for Friday prayers. The women immediately told their husbands in irate and aggrieved tones what they had heard. The men did not believe that the weak and emaciated Rida could be capable of such feats, and those who had not believed in the reality of the jinn were now compelled to admit they were wrong. They now believed Rida had invisible jinn brothers who rushed to his rescue whenever he needed help. They started walking more and more in dark alleyways and hanging around ruins and cemeteries, in the hope of making friends with someone who would rescue them and help them raise their heads in front of their wives.

30

Mazin was sitting in his room, not giving much thought to the hot night that made him pour with sweat. He was following a soccer match being broadcast live on one of the television stations when his mother came in and turned it off, paying no attention to his cries of protest. She informed him in an exhausted voice that she was tired of lying. She said she wasn't his mother but his sister, that she was only five years older than him and that his father, whom he did not remember, was the one who had asked her while breathing his last not to leave her brother in need of a mother. Mazin was sad because he had lost a kind mother, but he was also happy because he had gained an older sister. "Do you know that I always wondered how my mother could be so close to me in age," he asked, "and when I didn't find an answer I always said God was capable of anything?"

Mazin felt the blood boiling in his veins. His body was tense and yearning for a lot of water. He rushed to the bathroom, took off his clothes, and stood under the shower, from which poured a powerful stream of water. His sister followed him, to let him know that she was tired of lying, that she was not his sister but a stranger and an orphan who had been raised together with him. She then welcomed her surrender to the water.

31

Maha celebrated her fiftieth birthday. A few weeks later, she became aware of the young man her husband had hired as the new chauffeur for his car. She felt annoyed with herself for her forgetfulness and her embarrassing mistakes, and set about celebrating her thirtieth birthday. Her friends whispered that next year Maha will celebrate her twenty-ninth birthday. When her husband gave her a genuine fur coat for a present, she asked his driver, "What kind of present do you give your wife on her birthday?"

The driver seemed taken aback by the question, but lost no time in answering, "The poor woman I'll marry won't celebrate her birthday because she won't know what day she was born."

Maha's husband let her know he was traveling on urgent business which couldn't be postponed and was delighted to see that she received the news of his departure with dejection and suffering. She said she'd desert her own car for the duration of his absence and would use his instead so as to keep him in her thoughts the whole time. When he returned from his travels, he asked if she had used his car. She stretched lazily, and said, "Twice a day, or more.

You driver is very familiar with the city, and he knows the shortest and most beautiful routes."

She suggested her husband pay the driver handsomely for the many extra hours, but the driver resigned without giving an excuse when he learned his employer was going to be traveling again. A different chauffeur took his place, one who was careful about his health and did not swallow a mouthful of food until after he had chewed it very, very slowly and it begged to him to hurry up and swallow.

32

Darwish was a man who had no skill in life other than teaching reading and writing to the young, but he hated his profession and hated children: he saw them as dissemblers who had enough cunning to appear innocent. He fell in love with a dancer, in front of whom he would falter in his speech like a child trying to speak his first words. His love increased when he saw how modest she was when she appeared in public fully dressed. He asked for help from his friends, who made fun of him behind his back and vied with each other in offering a steady stream of advice. One such piece of advice was that a woman likes to be given roses. Darwish thought over his friends' words, but their advice did not appeal to him. He gave the dancer a revolver of the most up-to-date design. She took it and contemplated it in silence, then suddenly said to Darwish, "Do you know what I would do if I knew how to use this revolver?" He shook his head. She said, "I would shoot you. Then you'd be at rest, and so would I."

He told his friends what happened, but they quickly drew his attention to the fact that her concern for his rest was a sign that she loved him but was too embarrassed to admit it. They said a woman loves a forceful and tough man, and he must now convince her he was forceful and tough. And no sooner did Darwish see the dancer in the lounge where she worked than he slapped her without provocation, but he came away with his head bloody from the blows it had received from a shoe with a stiletto heel. He complained to his friends, but they expressed surprise at his simple-mindedness: it was obvious she loved him because for his sake she had sacrificed an expensive heel. They encouraged him to keep after her, reminding him that a woman loves an honorable man who wants to get married and start a family. Darwish followed their advice and insisted that the dancer marry him. She had had enough of his nagging and agreed. She enticed him into abandoning teaching and taking up another profession which required hardly any capital, was not dangerous, and whose profits were guaranteed.

33

The youth went wild when he heard the four men cursing the neighborhood where he lived. He pulled a knife and attacked them, but in a few moments he was down on the ground. One of the four men looked at him and said to his friends, laughing, "Look! Better looking than a woman! We made a mistake. We shouldn't have stabbed him with our daggers."

Everyone in the neighborhood – men, women, and children – walked in the funeral of the murdered youth. At the cemetery, when his coffin was placed on the ground next to the open grave, the wailing and crying rose to a pitch. Aisha al-Ghayyash did not wail and cry but quietly focused her attention on the man standing behind her who was taking advantage of the crowd of mourners to press against her back. She felt that his clinging was having an effect, making him breathe harder. She pretended she was not paying any attention but was absorbed in the scene in front of her. She bent forward the moment the corpse was lifted from the coffin and stayed that way, expecting the man not to be satisfied merely with pressing against her but would hurry to take advantage of what he had inadvertently started. But he lost his nerve and turned into a wall. She could no longer hide her disappointment, turned around, and gave him an irritated and disapproving look. The man was none other than her husband. After an embarrassing moment which passed quickly, she shouted at him in an angry and rebuking voice: "Is this how you harass the daughters of the people, as if you had no wife?"

He asked her to lower her voice, but she ignored him and insisted that, from his smell and the sound of his breathing, she had known who it was the moment he stood behind her but she wanted to test him, and he had failed the test. He swore to her as they walked home that he was fooling around with her only because he knew that she knew who he was. But she was not convinced and kept her face in a frown, feeling angry and insulted. She broke into tears the moment they came into the house. She rushed into the bedroom and threw herself on the bed. Her husband followed, trying to mollify her. She surrendered to him, still complaining and making no effort to wipe away her tears. She found herself reliving her slow movement in the funeral procession, her standing among the graves, and the clinging of the man behind her. She was bending down, pretending she just wanted to see the corpse being lifted from the coffin and laid into the grave. She was expecting the man to go further in what he had started, but did not have an opportunity to turn around and face him indignantly. The eyes of the mourners were filled with tears, and she saw nothing more than the murdered youth wrapped in his shroud and disappearing into the grave.

34

The director of the government hospital did not let anyone know he was starting his nightly rounds. He went into one of the rooms and found that a male nurse had a female patient on the floor and was lying on top of her. The nurse said to the director in a welcoming tone and without stopping, "Do come in, doctor."

The patient had closed her eyes out of shame or pleasure, or maybe she had fainted. The nurse noticed the director's look of astonishment, and said without stopping, "There's no need to wonder. Unlike many others, I don't like beds."

The director left in shock and went into another room, which was larger and lined with metal beds painted white. He was surprised to see that many patients had surrounded a young man of twenty and were setting on him with slaps and blows, saying the whole time, "Talk! Admit it!"

But the young man was crying without shame, letting tears flow down his face and swearing in a pleading voice that he was suffering from cancer, that he was going to die in four weeks and had nothing to hide or confess. The patients then informed the director that the young man was not sick but had been planted by the police in order to spy on them and discover their political leanings. Puzzled, the director left the room, only to see in the corridor two female nurses who had pinned to the wall a young doctor with fair complexion and blond hair and were feeling him with wanton fingers. One of them said to the frowning director, "This poor fellow is a patient who hasn't said what's wrong with him, and we're examining him."

The director muttered some vague words and hurried down the corridor. He went into the first room he chanced upon but was immediately struck by a strong and disgusting smell that came from an old man who was lying motionless in a bed, his eyes glazed in a fixed stare and his ashen face contorted by a searing and unbearable pain. The doctor hurried out with frightened steps. He did not finish his rounds and wanted to scream in reproach until his voice went hoarse. He went into a room set aside for physicians, but found four doctors drinking beer and smoking cigarettes. They did not stand up out of respect, nor did they seem to have taken any notice of him but kept staring avidly at the television. He stood a few moments in a state of speechless confusion. Then he sat in a chair facing the television set and, with eyes wide open, he saw the most modern jet fighters dropping huge sacks full of wheat and sugar on top of ancient mud houses scattered over a barren landscape. Every time a sack landed, it brought the roof down on its dwellers and buried them in rubble covered with mountains of wheat and sugar. The jets hit their targets with precision, and the doctors cried out in admiration at the skill of the pilots while the director muttered "God is great!" in a subdued and terrified voice.

35

Iqbal al-Tabbakh divorced her husband after she caught him with her maid in a situation that was incompatible with modesty. "If you had betrayed me with a woman who was more beautiful than me," she said to him, "whose family more eminent than mine, whose education better, and whose car more luxurious, I would not have been angry and would have found a thousand excuses for you. But that you should betray me with a servant who is old and ugly and whose smell is repulsive is something I do not understand. It will perplex me until the day I die."

Her husband laughed and said, "And where is all your intelligence? Have you forgotten that he who eats baklava every day will find it boring and will enjoy eating rubbish?"

When a new law was proclaimed giving women the right to vote and run for parliament, Iqbal al-Tabbakh was the first woman to put herself forward as a candidate, regardless of the difficulties she would face. Women supported her enthusiastically, for she was subject to the same male oppression, rage, and baseness. She was one of them and could be their resounding voice. Male support was lukewarm at first but quickly turned to boundless enthusiasm when Iqbal started to meet with the men separately, one after the other. She presented her arguments slowly but surely, convincing them of the validity of her thoughts and opinions with irrefutable evidence and a logic so clear that no one could resist it. Those on their way out of her house warned those coming in that awaiting them was a fire which burned but did not kill and which would drive them to ask to be burned again.

When Iqbal al-Tabbakh's electoral victory was announced, her supporters and helpers broke into trills of joy, but Iqbal complained because she was obliged to wear clothes. Yet her complaints dwindled when she remembered that in the parliament she would be facing fierce and powerful enemies whom she would not be able to overcome except by resorting to her irrefutable arguments and her easy but inimitable logic, which could not be resisted or defeated.

36

Mukhtar al-Kahhal left no doctor of any renown without seeking a cure for an extreme weakness that made him very forgetful and unable to save himself from embarrassing situations unsuitable to his position in society. Imported as well as local drugs failed to cure him, and he remained prey to his infirmity. But when he glimpsed Rasha, the young woman who walked on the ground as if she were flying, he jumped like one who had come into contact with boiling water. He forgot that he was sixty, had been married four times without producing children, and that each marriage had ended in divorce and mutual recrimination. He wanted to marry Rasha as quickly as possible, and her family enthusiastically welcomed the match for he was well connected, belonged to an old family, and his wealth was beyond measure.

Mukhtar al-Kahhal's forgetfulness was infectious, for all those with whom he came into contact became forgetful like him. Rasha's parents forgot to consult her about the person she was about to marry, and Rasha forgot to reproach them because they did not consult her about the man who was going to be her life-partner and whom she was going to be looking at day and night.

As he had wished, Mukhtar al-Kahhal married Rasha in the quickest possible time and his neighbors whispered that an abundance of wealth turned a skeleton into a champion of champions.

When a month had passed after their marriage, Mukhtar al-Kahhal bought many sheep, had them slaughtered, and distributed fresh meat to the poor and the unfortunate to celebrate the pregnancy of Rasha. But he prevented her from consulting any doctors and charged a trusty old woman from the Kahhal family with taking care of her and looking after her pregnancy. After nine months Rasha gave birth to a boy with blond hair, and Mukhtar distributed generously of his wealth to those in need, and they called upon heaven to grant him a new baby every year. The midwife, however, found it strange that the child looked very much like Dr. Abdel Ghani al-Muzayyab, and she looked up to heaven with piety, acknowledging that God was indeed omnipotent.

The following year, Rasha gave birth to a boy with black, hair that was coarse and stiff, and the midwife wondered about chance occurrences that made the child look like Qasim al-Tayyan, the construction worker. She was content to say that the Creator can do as He sees fit.

The third year, Rasha gave birth to a daughter with very fair skin, large greenish eyes, and fine black hair. The old midwife was surprised that the girl resembled the pharmacist Abbas al-Hakim, and she said that the Creator was master and his creatures nothing more than slaves created in order to be obedient.

The fourth year, Rasha gave birth to a boy who was tall and thin, and had a big nose. The old midwife marveled at the strange resemblance between him and the new chief of police, and she murmured that God metes out rewards without reckoning the cost.

When what the old midwife was saying about the resemblance of his children to other men reached his ears, Mukhtar al-Kahhal sent after her and threatened to cut off her tongue if she continued spreading her rumors. But she was not intimidated. She stuck her tongue out and said: "Here! Cut it off!"

"You blame me," she added irritably, "yet no one deserves blame except your father, God have mercy on his soul. He was wild about married women, and made many conquests. No woman was safe from him, and if God had not ordered us to protect honor, I would have told you all that I knew. The mothers of Dr. Muzayyab, al-Tayyan, the pharmacist, and the chief of police were your father's lovers. He was given choice morsels of meat, and their husbands got bones, nagging, and grumbling.

Mukhtar al-Kahhal was pleased with what he heard and the earth seemed to him to be a land of intimacy, full of brothers whom he did not know and who did not know him.

The fifth year, Rasha became pregnant but she died in childbirth. Yet the old woman was certain that if the unborn child had been destined to live, he would have looked like Adli al-Mahmoud, who moved from one state of idle joblessness to another. The old woman then declared that God was wise and merciful.

37

The television weatherman announced that heavy rain would fall that night, and the advertisement following the news declared that effervescent Vitamin C was the best protection against the common cold. The woman announcer who came on the screen after the commercial said the film was a crime thriller and wished the viewers an enjoyable evening of viewing. As she was leaving the studio, one of the employees informed her that the director of the station wanted to see her right away. She rushed anxiously to his office. The director asked her to sit down and pointed to a cup of coffee near her. He said he had ordered it for her ahead of time and spoke at length, praising her style of delivery. He said it was distinguished and attractive. He spoke of her hair and said her hairdresser deserved a generous reward. He spoke of her eyes and said the expression in them was that of an unassuming queen. And he spoke of her body with the words of an expert who was not satisfied only with speaking. The announcer closed her eyes and said to the director in a low, trembling voice.

"What are you doing?"

"Guess," he answered.

"I can't guess," she said.

"Try again," said the director. "There's no need to hurry." The announcer then followed his advice. She did not try to open her eyes. After all, it was a rainy night and the crime thriller was scary and full of victims, and she had seen it anyway.

38

Sayf al-Qattan wanted to rise from his chair and leave the coffee house the moment he glimpsed the woman he chased walking along the sidewalk, as she did every morning on her way to work. But he was astonished to find that he remained stuck to the chair, and that the legs of the chair were also glued to the floor. It occurred to him to call the waiter and ask for help, but he changed his mind when he considered that the waiter might draw the attention of the other customers to his plight, saying to them, "It appears that the honored gentleman is going to be our guest for an indefinite period."

Thus, Sayf al-Qattan was obliged to remain in his chair close to the glass front of the coffee house. As he stared speechlessly at the street crowded with people and cars, he ordered a cup of coffee and drank it, a cup of tea and drank it, and bought a newspaper and a magazine and read them to the last letter. Every once in a while he would try to get up from his chair, but in vain. When it was nearly two o'clock, he focused his attention on the street, expecting the woman to come that way on her way back from work, and he was not disappointed. She did pass by, walking her slow gait with a bearing that exuded pride. But today her eyes were different, for they gave him a long look that did not hide a frank and hot appeal he had not noticed before. He tried to rise from the chair, and, to his surprise, he could do so without hindrance. He rushed out of the coffee house and followed her, always making sure to stay a few meters behind, as was his custom every day. Suddenly, the woman halted while he continued walking, his face frozen and feeling embarrassed, and no sooner had he come close than she started screaming angrily at him, reviling him for his pursuit. Very quickly, a number of men who were ready to help the woman gathered around her. One of them asked, pointing to Sayf al-Qattan: "Has he done anything improper?"

"Every morning and afternoon," the woman answered without hesitation, "he follows me and asks me to go home with him, claiming his family is away on a journey. But today he reached for my hand and tried to drag me to his house against my will."

Her lying stunned Sayf al-Qattan and he tried to say something, but the man gave him a ringing slap on the face, and said angrily, "Shut up, you dog! Do you still have a tongue that can speak!"

That slap was just the beginning. The other men took part in slapping, hitting, and kicking him, and in spite of the painful blows descending on him Sayf could see the woman he admired standing there with her lips wide open as though she were panting. Her hand was on her neck in the gesture of one who appeared to be choking, and from her eyes came the same hot appeal. Sayf then called out to the men beating him. He urged them to hit him hard, but they thought he was mocking them and beat him harder and harder. From that time Sayf became a bitter and savage man who was obliged to spend his time in hospitals and graveyards.

39

Mazhar al-Huseini believed his wife had strange and hidden attributes that were confusing and beyond explanation, comprehensible only to someone who had lived with her. Every time he embraced her, he received a piece of good news that changed his life. He was embracing her with delicacy and care the moment he learned he had been appointed general manager of a state-owned company with a huge annual budget and indolent accountants. He was giving her a well-behaved and modest embrace when news reached him that he had been chosen as Finance Minister. And he was giving her a mean and violent embrace when it was announced in the newscast on television that he had been chosen as Prime Minister. And he was hugging her as a child hugs a cat when it was reported to him that the whole country had elected him President of the Republic.

Mazhar al-Huseini never spoke of his wife's attributes, making sure they remained a secret. But one night, when he had drunk enough alcohol to feel everything spinning around him, he admitted to some of his close friends the secret role his wife had played in his success, and they kept their silence. They did not tell him they had embraced their wives and embraced his wife, but with no improvement in their condition. He noticed that they did not agree with what he had said and he tried to convince them but did not succeed. He returned to his palace in distress and rushed to embrace his wife, eager for her tender flesh. At that moment, his secretary called to tell him that what she had to say couldn't wait till morning. In a trembling and submissive voice she informed him that he had been granted American citizenship.

40

Hani Abdel Muttalib celebrated his thirtieth birthday in his small room. He hugged his pillow while licking his lips and imagined it was the actress Sharon Stone meowing.

He stood in front of the mirror and imagined he was addressing some beautiful women who were put off by his stinginess. He said to them, "I'm the one who will propose what demands you can make."

He went into the bathroom, washed his face and hands with soap and water and imagined the world's generals crowding the door with cotton towels in hand.

He leaned against the wall and imagined it was the last remaining wall on earth.

He sat on the old sofa and imagined the world's rich standing in front of him with their heads bowed, asking for advice on how to keep their millions, and he made it a condition that every word he uttered had an exorbitant and non-negotiable price. He also imagined that all the scientists on earth were rushing to his door asking for advice, and he said to them, "I have only one piece of advice, and that is, you should immediately forget reading and writing."

He drank some cold water and imagined it was well-aged whiskey. He walked out of his room, went into the street, and staggered onto the sidewalk. He then leaned with both his hands against the trunk of a tree and threw up, regretting having drunk too much.

41

Abdel Hadi placed the watermelon with the green skin in a large platter and said to himself as he was preparing to cut into it: "If it's red, I'll marry Suha. In exactly one year, we'll differ and separate after a long battle in the courts. But if it's pale, Suha will marry me, and I won't even be able to breathe without asking her permission."

He cut the watermelon in two, and found its flesh a pale yellow. "This being the case," he said to himself, "I'll stay a bachelor."

He held the telephone receiver close to his ear and tried to call his friend Abdallah, saying to himself, "If I find him at home, I'll go to a cinema and watch a detective film, but if he's not at home I'll hang around in the streets for an hour, not a minute more or a minute less."

Abdallah was not at home. His mother said he had gone to his sister's house to reconcile her with her husband. Abdel Hadi left his house and wandered the streets, saying to himself, "If I get tired, I'll go into a coffee house and smoke a narghile. If I don't, I'll eat something in a restaurant."

He roamed the streets for an hour without getting tired. So he went into a restaurant and ordered a skewer of meat and a salad, saying to himself, "If the meat's tender, I'll go ahead and vote tomorrow, but if it's tough, I'll follow the first woman I meet on the street."

The waiter brought the meat, the salad, and the bread, and the meat was as tough as leather. Abdel Hadi felt disgusted and did not eat it. He ate only the bread and the salad, and left the restaurant. The first woman he saw on the street had a lovely face and beautiful figure. He came close to her and felt her buttocks, but she rushed to complain to a policeman nearby. Abdel Hadi said to himself: "If the policemen arrests me, I'll volunteer to give blood in two days, but if he only gives me a slap to teach me manners, I'll go to the baths in the souk tonight."

The policeman did not arrest or slap him. He gave the woman a searching and admiring look and said, "He's right. Anyone who sees all this beauty would not be able to control himself."

Abdel Hadi stood immobilized in the street, at a loss what to do and unable to find anything to say to himself.

42

If Iffat said the sun was black, her husband Taha would not disagree. He trusted her so completely that he would look at the yellow sun and say it was black. But his family thought differently. His sister saw Iffat as a lizard or a scorpion. His first brother saw her merely as a woman who knew how to make use of what she had. His second brother saw her as lucky because she had married a child whose body had matured but whose mind had not. And his father with the wagging tongue was not happy that his son was submissive to Iffat when he was better looking, softer, and more feminine than she was. As for his mother, she could not bear to hear Iffat's name after Taha left home and went to live with his wife. She used to say, "The mistake is ours. We married him off when he was still too young and had no idea what the world was like. The moment he could breathe in the scent of a woman he lost his head and forgot his family. He was like someone who had nothing and had fallen into a basket full of treats."

Taha enjoyed being submissive. He saw Iffat as a most beautiful woman, a woman whose beauty was more radiant when she felt content, and this radiance tempted him to long for her while at work. And when, without prior warning, he received a notice laying him off for no reason, he was not angry or unhappy. He secretly welcomed what had happened because it gave him the opportunity to be near Iffat day and night. But one day she said to him in a vexed manner that betrayed her irritation, "Stop looking at me the way a hungry cat looks at a piece of meat. I'm not made of steel."

She asked him to look for some entertainment outside the house, but he said without hesitation that she was the only person in the whole world who could keep him amused. She then suggested in a mocking voice that he go out and play with the boys in the street, but he asked, stunned, "What kind of a strange suggestion is that? What will people say about me when they see a young man playing with little boys in the street?"

But Iffat answered spitefully, "As long as you enjoy staying at home, not looking for work and forgetting you're responsible for a family, there's nothing more suitable for you than playing with little boys."

Taha rose from his chair feeling angry for the first time since they married. He walked out of his third-floor apartment in a hurry and, as he came down the stairs, strange sounds that roused his curiosity reached his ears. He looked down from above, and in front of a door on the first floor there were two people whom he knew. He had assumed all along they were brother and sister. The boy, who was no more than twelve years old, held very tightly a girl who was even younger than him. He gripped her hips with both his hands, and the girl made no effort to push him off but tried to get even closer, as if she wanted them to be one creature. Taha coughed artificially, and the two became aware of him. The girl rushed inside the house and slammed the door behind her with as much force as she could muster, while the boy remained standing there with his feet apart, his body tense, and his face red. "Salaam," Taha said, lingering over the word.

The boy did not respond to his greeting, but gave him a defiant look. Taha ignored him and kept walking down the stairs, overcome, without knowing why, by a feeling of embarrassment which he disliked.

Taha walked out of the main gate of the building to find there were no children playing in the street. He walked slowly and aimlessly on the sidewalk under dusty green trees. He was not angry with Iffat but blamed himself because he had not drawn her out about the mistake he made the night before that made her so nervous and ill-tempered in the morning. He had not been walking long when his gaze fell upon a coffin surrounded by men, women, and children who were lamenting and crying, even though there was no corpse in it. He imagined that in a few moments they would descend upon anyone walking in the street and put him in it. With quickening steps he put some distance between himself and them. When he felt tired and walked more slowly, he noticed a man looking out of a window on the first floor of a building of white stone, speaking to a boy with fair complexion near the entrance to the building. He was saying, "Come inside the house, and you won't regret it."

The boy was frozen in his place like someone sulking, and Taha said to him, "Can't you hear your father calling?"

"Not my father," said the boy hastily.

"Your brother?"

"Not my brother, or my uncle, or my mother, or a relative of mine."

"Young man," the man called out in an angry voice, "Better go your way and leave that boy alone, or else I'll call the police."

Taha continued on his way, taking care not to look like someone who was running away in fear. He moved from one street to another, pouring with sweat, until he reached a new avenue that was lined with modern buildings, some of which were finished but empty while others looked unfinished and uninhabited. He was surprised to come upon some men engaged in a violent fight, paying no heed to the policemen who were trying to stop them from hitting each other. Taha then observed a tall man with broad shoulders, protruding eyeballs, and a thick mustache looking searchingly at him. Taha looked at him in fascination and revulsion. The stranger smiled and approached him. He asked what the fight was about and Taha answered without any hesitation that he didn't know. "How can it be possible that you don't know?" asked the man, doubting his words.

Taha become confused and said nothing. The stranger then put his sweaty hand around Taha's neck and said, frowning, "You do know what the fight's about, but you're not telling me."

Taha became more confused and said in a halting voice that he didn't know the cause of the quarrel. He felt the angry fingers of the man pressing tightly against his neck. "Are you accusing me of being stupid?" he said irately. "You know the reason but you're not telling me."

Taha did not answer. He watched the policemen as they began to arrest those involved in the fight and drag them to the police cars. The stranger then said to Taha, "Aren't you ashamed? Why are you gazing at the police as if they've just killed your mother? Is this the reward of those who serve the people?"

"On the contrary. I like the police and respect their profession."

"You're a liar. You, like others, don't like policemen. You're lying, but you're trying to humor me by saying you like them."

"Listen," said Taha impatiently. "You don't know me, and I don't know you. There's no reason to be talking to me."

He tried to get away, but the stranger prevented him. He held Taha's neck tightly with his powerful fingers, and said in a threatening voice, "Let's go! Come with me, or else you'll be sorry."

"Where?" asked Taha. "To the police station?"

The stranger did not answer, but led him to the basement of an unfinished and empty building nearby. Once inside, he did not speak of the fight or the police. When Taha had an opportunity to leave the building, he found himself stumbling along, remembering with shame what had happened to him on the floor of the basement. He remembered asking the stranger, "Why are you carrying a revolver?"

The stranger laughed and said, "So that what I'm doing to you won't be done to me."

Taha felt hungry and thought it was strange. He took from his pocket a piece of chocolate which the stranger had given him, and was about to toss it to the ground in disgust. But the hand that held the chocolate lifted it to his mouth and pushed it inside, and his teeth chewed it until it was mixed with saliva. Taha was amazed at what his hand had done, and decided not to honor his promise to the stranger to come to the building at the same time the following day.

He was surprised by his feeling of pride when the stranger said that he was handsome and delectible. He wished his wife could hear that, and kept on walking about in the streets, until he felt tired. He went into the first coffee house he saw and started smoking cigarettes and drinking coffee. An old man with short gray hair and a face that looked like an upside-down pear came over and asked his permission to sit with him. Taha welcomed him with agitation and surprise, as most of the tables in the coffee shop were empty.

The old man said to Taha that the weather today was hot even though the forecast last night had predicted it would be cool. He added as he looked at the rummy players around the coffee house that gambling was more dangerous than narcotics because a drug addict may be cured but there is no cure for an addicted gambler. He said that, as usual, he hadn't eaten that morning and was sorry because he now felt hungry. Taha asked about his work, and he said he was now retired. He used to be a merchant but repented and went on the hajj twice so that God might forgive all the lies he had to tell in order to make his business a success. Taha then asked him what his sons did. "I have no sons and daughters," he said as he looked at Taha in amazement. "God save us from the troubles of sons and daughters! I have never been married. May God save us from women's evil!"

The old man gazed sorrowfully at the customers in the coffee house and said that most of his friends had died and those still alive were struggling with death.

Taha noticed that the waiter was signaling him secretly to come over. He left his table, saying he had to wash his hands, and went to see the waiter, who immediately asked, "Who's that man sitting with you?"

"I don't know him," Taha answered, "and he doesn't know me. And it's not me who's sitting with him, but rather it's he who's sitting with me."

The waiter said, "You fool! This man is well known. He has killed no less than ten people."

"If what you say is true," asked Taha, "then why hasn't he been imprisoned or hanged?"

"I don't know," answered the waiter, "He who spreads unbelief is not necessarily an infidel. I'm only passing on what I heard about him. But be careful. I advise you not to make him angry."

Taha went back to his table and offered the old man a cigarette, which he took with thanks. He talked about his dead mother, whom he had seen in a dream wearing white clothes and whose body exuded beautiful scents. He asked for an explanation of his dream, and Taha said there was only one explanation, that his mother was alive in Paradise. The old man was pleased, and asked, "Are there coffee shops in Paradise?"

Taha answered with confidence, "There are coffee shops and restaurants, and they're free."

The old man was even more pleased, and asked, "And what else is there in Paradise?"

"In Paradise," answered Taha, "there's all that your heart desires. If you want to see a dove, then immediately a dove will appear and circle around you. If you want to see a cat, the cat will come into being especially for you. It will come meowing and rub against your feet. And if you desire a woman with particular qualities, then she will be created immediately and will rush to do everything that pleases you."

"Holy God! You've made me long for Paradise. Even if my destiny is to be in hell, I'll run away to Paradise."

The waiter resumed his obscure signaling with some urgency, but Taha said goodbye to the old man, who thanked him warmly because he had given him the opportunity to talk, though he had almost forgotten how to speak. He left the coffee house in a hurry, ignoring the waiter's signals. He walked till nighttime, took a bus that passed by his house and sat next to a woman dressed in black. She gazed at him in amazement. He felt annoyed by her staring and asked her derisively, "Is it forbidden to sit here?"

The woman smiled sadly and said, "No, not at all. I keep looking at you because you look like my son Nabil. May God have mercy on his soul!"

"May God have mercy on all of us!" Taha said.

The woman wiped her eyes and nose with a handkerchief made of yellow cloth. "When did your son die?" asked Taha.

"Four days ago," the woman answered.

"And how did he die?" asked Taha.

"In all his life," the woman answered, "he was not sick once. He went to sleep one night, and when we came to wake him up in the morning we found him dead."

"And how old was he?" Taha asked.

"About your age," the woman answered, "or younger by a few months."

The conductor approached Taha, and the woman insisted on paying his fare. He didn't object and thanked her. "God be praised!" she said in a voice filled with awe. "Even your voice sounds like his."

She gave him her address, and asked him to visit so that her husband could meet him. He was so sad over the loss of his son that he couldn't sleep at night. Taha promised to come as quickly as possible, and she kept talking to him about her son until he felt he knew him, and felt genuine sorrow for his death.

When he returned home on the third floor, he found Iffat waiting anxiously. She asked why he was late, but he just stared at her, silently wondering why he hadn't noticed before the sheer imbecility hiding in her big eyes. She asked him to give her an answer immediately and stop acting like a pampered, sulking boy, but he ignored her and let her bombard him with questions without his uttering a single word. She became angry and rushed into the bedroom, slamming the door behind her violently. Taha smiled scornfully and went out to the balcony, longing for some fresh air. He noticed an open window on the first floor and saw two women in bed exchanging hot kisses as if they were a man and a woman. One of them noticed him and carried on more intently with what she was doing. He had no chance to observe further what was taking place behind the open window, as the light in the room was turned off, but he could still hear the women laughing. He went back to his living room and sat down on his favorite couch in front of the television and remembered what had happened to him. He refused to accept his surrender to the strange man and decided to go back the next day to the cellar of that building at the agreed time, carrying a knife big enough to slaughter an ox. He smiled happily because his hand was going to let go of the knife as soon as the strange man arrived. He slept soundly, a sleep full of comforting dreams. His wife woke him up in the morning. She was frowning as she said he was late for work, but he stared at her as if he did not know her and went back to sleep. He saw a dead man laid out in an uncovered coffin set on the ground in a souk crowded with buyers and sellers, but no one was noticing him.

Taha gasped in fright the moment he saw the face of the murdered man. He wanted to wake up, but he remained sleeping.

43

Samira al-Ghuss burst suddenly into the bedroom and found Radwan lying on the bed, his eyes red, gaping at the pages of a magazine full of naked women. Her angry shouting resounded throughout the house. Radwan immediately tore up the magazine and promised Samira that until the day he died he would touch only magazines that showed pictures of men. Samira did not stop reproaching and mocking him, and he threatened to throw a tantrum and leave for his parent's house. "Up and go then! No one is stopping you."

Radwan rubbed his eyes with his fingers, and said to Samira, "Since you're fed up with me to such an extent, why don't you take a break from having to look at me and allow me to go to a coffee house?"

"Have you washed the dishes?" asked Samira.

"I washed them," he answered. "And while you were sleeping I also washed the spoons, forks, and knives."

"And cleaned the house?" she asked.

"Look around you," said Radwan, "and you'll see that the house sparkles like a mirror. I cleaned it while you were bathing."

"You can go to the coffee house," said Samira, "as long as you're away only for sixty minutes. Be careful not to come back even one second late."

Radwan then rushed towards Samira and tried to kiss her cheek, but she pushed him away in disgust and said in a voice heavy with reproach, "There's no need for these ridiculous movements. I know you and know that you can't stand me and wish I were dead."

Radwan said in a trembling and disapproving voice, "God save us! If I can't stand you, what obliges me to stay at home?"

"You stay at home," said Samira, "because you want to keep me ill at ease."

Radwan went back to sitting on the bed and said, "I won't go to the coffee house as long as you're not pleased with me."

"You'll go," she said, "whether you like it or not."

Radwan left the house, and came back fifty-six minutes later. He was shocked to find the place full of policemen. They informed him his wife had been killed, and he gasped in horror and died for a few moments, then came back to life, feeling full of regret. He walked barefoot on broken glass and cried without tears because he would no longer be looking at her black hair and fair skin or hearing her angry voice. He asked to look at her but was told her body had been taken to the hospital. He felt a secret pleasure that made him ashamed, and he disowned it. He tried to repress this pleasure or even get rid of it, but its power grew in spite of him, forcing his lips to smile. The police watched him intently with a curiosity that turned into a suspicion which saw Radwan's smile as merry laughter. He became aware of their staring but swore while laughing that it was impossible for him to have killed his wife. They arrested him anyway and accused him of killing her. He was surprised and sad in turn. He laughed and cried, and did not deny their accusation. He confessed what he had done, and asked the policeman who was putting the handcuffs around his wrists, "How was she killed. Was she strangled, or stabbed with a knife?"

The policeman said nothing and pushed him roughly into a speeding car which took him to the station. As soon as the interrogator saw the handcuffed young man and knew what he was charged with, his face turned red. He bit his lower lip and ordered the policemen to release him immediately and leave the room. When they were alone, he said to Radwan in apologetic tones, "Don't mind them. They're ignorant, and carry on as if the murder of a wife were a crime. All of us wish to get rid of our women, but some of us are brave while others are worthless cowards. Please allow me to express my admiration of your manliness, for our prisons are full of people who deny all they did, claiming they are innocent victims."

He invited Radwan to sit in a chair next to his desk and said, "No need for tension and nervousness. Come now, relax as if you were at home. We're not in a hurry. We have all the time we need. I have only one question to ask, 'Why, and how, did you kill your wife?'"

Radwan answered, "When I returned home, my dinner was cold and my wife wasn't waiting for me as she does every day. I looked for her and found her in the bedroom, which was full of drunken men, and she was jumping merrily from one lap into another. I was angry beyond words. I unsheathed my knife and fell upon her and cut her throat from one jugular vein to the other."

The interrogator then said, "You wife was not killed with a knife. Stop beating around the bush, wasting your time and mine."

Radwan said, "The truth is that I had lunch at home with my wife as usual. After lunch we drank coffee together and discussed politics. My wife hates the government like death, and I love the government. I couldn't bear her mocking the government, for when she mocks the government she's mocking me. And I'm a man who doesn't accept being mocked by a woman. So I threw myself at her and choked her with both hands. Take a look at my fingers. They're capable of choking a raging bull."

The interrogator said, "Have some honor and stop lying! Your wife wasn't strangled."

Radwan said, "I just remembered. She wanted a new dress, even though the one she was wearing was still new. I bought it five years ago. I tried to convince her of the damage caused by excessive spending and wasting money, but she wouldn't be convinced. She kept insisting on buying a new dress. I'm not stupid enough to squander my resources on useless things, so I poured gasoline on her and burned her to death."

The interrogator said, "You're a shameless liar. Your wife did not die by burning."

Radwan said in confusion, "I was in fact lying. Now I will speak the truth. I got bored with my wife and could no longer stand to look at her face or hear her voice. So I swore three times that I would divorce her, but she refused to leave the house and go back to her family. She clung to me, moaning and crying and swore she would never leave me as long as she lived. I felt she was a huge insect about to devour me and I shot her with my pistol seven times, and I estimate not one of those shots missed."

The interrogator said, "Your wife (May God have mercy on her soul!) died without your firing a single shot."

Radwan said, "I will tell you exactly what happened. I woke up in the morning and my coffee wasn't ready. I found my wife still stretching and yawning and listening to trivial songs on the radio, so I rushed at her and strung her up because I can't stand a lazy wife who doesn't respect her husband."

The interrogator said, "Damnation! Your wife did not die by hanging."

Radwan said, "Since she didn't die by hanging, she must have died from poisoning."

The interrogator said, "Aren't you ashamed to tell these lies? Don't you know that I'm well-known among my colleagues for my patience, but you have exhausted all the patience that I possess, and if our prison cells weren't already full, I would've stuck you in one of them for a month as punishment for your lying prattle and I wouldn't have allowed you to go back home now."

Radwan said in utter surprise, "It sounds as if you're telling me I'm not going to be put in prison."

"You won't be going to prison," said the interrogator. "You'll be sleeping at home."

"And my confessions?" asked Radwan.

"They're useless. Your brother-in-law has been arrested," the interrogator said. "A little while ago he confessed he killed her because she was living with you without being married."

"But we were living like a married couple," said Radwan. "It was she who refused to get married. She detested marriage and had a low opinion of married people."

The interrogator chuckled, and Radwan asked, "How did her brother kill her?"

The interrogator said, as he scratched his head with his right hand, "He carried her to the roof of the building and threw her over. It's clear she didn't resist him in the least. He also confessed that if he had found you at home, your fate would have been worse than hers."

Radwan was shocked. He imagined Samira with her head smashed, saying to him, "You didn't claim that you killed me, except to take away the pleasure of having the killer punished."

The interrogator then cautioned Radwan in a sarcastic tone. "Don't forget," he said, "the deceased has five brothers."

Radwan rose from his chair, bewildered and not knowing what to do. The policemen shoved him outside the station with aggressive and angry movements, and he walked in a street that was wet from pouring rain, imagining that someone was following him. He was frightened and ran in the rain until he reached his house. The moment he closed the door behind him he sighed with relief but was surprised by three of Samira's brothers, who emerged from the bedroom and descended upon him. They bound him with ropes, sealed his mouth with tape, and carried him to the roof. They dropped him to the street, and he fell like a big sock full of pebbles. The sock fell on hard ground and was ripped to pieces, and the pebbles, wet with blood, scattered all around and mixed with the rubbish in the street.

44

Zuhdi laughed as he lay back in front of the television set, convinced he would never again laugh this honest, ardent, and cheerful laughter even if he were to live two hundred years. His wife asked in surprise why he was laughing, but he kept laughing without answering. She said reproachfully, "Come on now. Let me know what's making you laugh like that so I can laugh like you and never part from you whether our days are sweet or bitter."

"Didn't you listen to the news a while ago?" asked Zuhdi.

"I listened from beginning to end," his wife said, "and there was nothing but news of catastrophes: floods, earthquakes, erupting volcanoes, and crashing civilian aircraft."

"But out of misfortune something good may come," said her husband. "The more catastrophes, the fewer people on earth, and that will hasten the day when I'll see what I've been hoping for: an earth without people, except for you and me. You'll be Eve, and I'll be Adam, and we'll bring forth a whole new line of human beings whose actions won't be deviant or corrupt – a line of descent that doesn't spring from a forbidden apple or from Cain and Abel."

She stared at him, as if seeing him for the first time. He ignored her gaze and resumed his laughter, expecting her to follow suit. But she did not laugh because she suddenly remembered the days when she was a shy young student whose friends mocked her because of shyness, making her more shy. She remembered the times when Zuhdi touched her with eager fingers and she was too shy to stop him or hold him back. He believed that her reddening face, her rising and troubled breathing and her resentful shudder were signs of approval, intoxication, and a desire for more. He would then lead her from a dark and deserted street to a room with a locked door, paying no attention to her imploring, hurried, and resentful muttering, until she finally felt obliged to accept marriage to someone who was a mixture of bear, wolf, and hedgehog. She remembered sadly that she was going to reach old age without ever knowing what love was. She remembered her body at night, a wild and lonely animal deserted by sleep, stretching and calling to any man except her husband. She remembered how ashamed she felt when he called to her and how she ran away, guarding her dignity and her grave and silent demeanor. She remembered her mother, who had died three years earlier, and she cried as if her mother had died three minutes ago. Zuhdi stopped laughing and asked, "Why are you crying? If you're not going to laugh with me, I'm ready to cry with you."

"Haven't you noticed," asked the wife, "that the catastrophes are lazy, slow, and merciful, and we may die before your wish comes true?"

"What can I do?" said Zuhdi. "The eye can see, but the hand can't reach."

"Aren't you ashamed of lying?" asked his wife with a scornful and a hostile look. "Is it only your hand that can't reach, or is there something else that can reach even less than your hand?"

Zuhdi felt confused, and his face fell. His wife laughed, secure in the knowledge that this night he would not try to laugh again, but would remain scowling.

45

Anisa implored sleep to stay away, for her husband was lying in the next room in his winding sheet ready for burial in a hole in the ground and he needed someone to keep him company during this long and lonely night. But sleep did not heed her call and became a dark sea from which there was no escape. In her sleep Anisa saw her husband lying on top of a woman sprawled on the ground, and she was astonished and felt as though she were burning. She imagined she knew that woman, who, with closed eyes, had surrendered to a man whose face was not able to hide its revulsion. She was angry to be cheated on, and opened her eyes as wide as she could, holding tightly to her husband in spite of his revulsion. Her flesh became a hot, moist mouth with quivering lips asking for cold water which it did not receive. Anisa saw in her sleep that she was screaming for help in a room with no door and no windows. She was being raped by a man whose face could not be seen and who was saying to her with a rasp in his voice that he was going to kill her. He did not say he loved her, and her forced screaming persisted until she suffocated.

46

There were three sofas on the living room carpet but Omar and Fawziya sat on one of them in very close contact as if the room were full of invisible guests vying for a place to sit. Omar sat silently next to Fawziya, who was reading a book and breathing as though the air in the room was about to run out. Suddenly, she closed the book, stood up, and threw it across the room with all her strength. It crashed against a large frame hanging on the wall and brought to the floor a photograph of an old man with resigned eyes, shattering both glass and frame. Omar chuckled and said to Fawziya, "Your father will be angry with you."

"Leave our father under the ground," Fawziya said. "Surely, he has enough to worry about. Yet he might feel sorry for me now because I've just finished reading the last book in the house and there's nothing left to read to amuse myself."

"You're not in need of anyone to feel sorry for you," Omar said in a serious voice, "Tomorrow, please God, the house will be full of new books. I'll steal a whole library and bring it home to you because I can't bear to see you unhappy."

"I've read a lot about mice munching on books," said Fawziya, "and all that is nothing but lies because mice can't stand books."

"And how did you find this out?" Omar asked in a surprised and questioning tone. "Did you question the mice?"

"It's obvious even to a blind man," answered Fawziya. "A few months ago, the house was full of mice, but they have run away, fearing they would starve to death. If they really liked books, they wouldn't have run away from a house filled with books but rather from one in which there was nothing fit to eat."

"Don't despair of God's mercy so quickly," Omar said in a quiet and confident voice. "Tomorrow, please God the Exalted, the house will be full of produce, and the mice will return."

"Are you going to win the lottery tomorrow?" Fawziya asked, mocking. "Or do you have a rich uncle in Brazil who has died and left you his fortune in bank accounts all over the world?"

"God willing, tomorrow I'll steal the grandest palace in this country."

"Will you steal its furniture, or only the pots and pans and cutlery?"

"God willing, I'll steal the whole palace, with its stones, windows and doors."

"A jar isn't always safe after a fall. The guards of these palaces are oppressive tyrants and will kill you."

"I won't be giving you the pleasure of crying over my corpse. I'll put them all to sleep, and they won't wake up till the Day of Judgment."

"Will you also steal the owner of the palace?"

"I'll bring him here all tied up and throw him at your feet."

"Don't you think that feeding him every day will need more than just a bit of money?"

"I'll leave him without food until he slowly loses weight and collapses, and the mice will thank me after devouring him with gusto."

"Your mission is fearful and difficult, and you'll need help. In a while it will be time for the noon prayer. I'll pray at noon, and call upon God to grant you success."

Omar was delighted with Fawziya's promise and relaxed further back on the sofa. He was confident of success because Fawziya's prayers were heard, as though the heavens were eager to please her. He closed his eyes, feeling refreshed. "Why don't you steal something we can eat now?" he heard Fawziya ask insistently.

Omar opened his eyes and said, "God willing, tomorrow I'll rob the richest orchard, and will bring you apricots, apples, grapes, pears, peaches, plums, and red and yellow melons."

"Stop talking now. Stop," said Fawziya, swallowing her spittle with difficulty. "You've aroused my appetite, and I'll end up eating you if you don't stop talking immediately."

"God willing, tomorrow I'll steal a young lamb which has just been slaughtered, and you'll eat its meat while it's still warm."

"I suggest you steal a donkey."

"Ugh! Donkey meat can't be chewed or digested."

"You'll need it to carry all the stuff you're going to steal."

"God willing, tomorrow I'll steal a whole herd of sheep, and you'll be eating meat morning, noon, and night."

"Doctors are cautioning people not to eat too much red meat. They advise us to eat more white meat."

"God willing, tomorrow I'll kidnap Nazha, our neighbor's wife. In all my life I've never seen a woman with such fair flesh."

"As of this moment, I'm giving up my share of her. You can eat her all by yourself."

Fawziya approached him. Her hands gripped his waist with firm fingers, and she asked, "What do you say to eating me right now?"

Omar answered, "God willing, I'll eat you tomorrow, after I've sprinkled you with salt and pepper."

Annoyed, her fingers released his waist and she bent down to the floor, picked up the book and started reading it again. But her voice kept on complaining.

47

Said kissed the lips of a beautiful and daring young woman. She complimented him on his kiss, saying without embarrassment that she enjoyed it and would welcome more, but she found fault with his dense mustache, in which the stale odor of tobacco had taken root, making it smell more like rotten fish. As soon as he reached home, Said rushed into the bathroom, paying no attention to his wife. He stood in front of the mirror and with a firm hand shaved his mustache. He then looked into the mirror and saw there a man he did not recognize. "Who are you?" he asked.

"My name is Raghid," said the man with the shaved mustache.

Raghid then laughed a merry and mocking laughter and said to Said, "The moment you shaved your mustache you disappeared. You didn't exist any more."

"Don't gloat or feel glad," Said said to Raghid. "In a few days my hair will grow back the way it was because it's very thick and has always given barbers a hard time."

Thereupon Raghid took hold of the scissors and set to cutting off the hair of his head. He covered the scalp with a thick layer of suds and shaved it clean, turning it into a shining pate, then said to Said, "Come! You're welcome to boast about your hair, now."

Raghid looked into the mirror in shock and saw a strange man whom he didn't recognize. Confused, he asked him in turmoil, "Who are you?"

"I'm Walid," said the man with the bald pate.

"There!" Said said to Raghid in a mocking voice. "You intended to do me harm, but you ended up hurting only yourself, for now the same thing has happened to you that happened to me."

Walid said to Raghid and Said, "Don't waste my time, you two. Admit you're both jackasses and leave me to do my work."

"And what is your work?" Raghid and Said asked with one voice.

"Have you forgotten that I'm married to the beautiful and intelligent Amal who's impossible to please?" Walid answered.

"She will kick you out the window," Said said, "for she loves my mustache and considers it a sign of true manhood."

"She loved my hair," said Raghid, "and used to pass her hand over it and say it was like the hair of a black stallion."

At that moment, Amal tried to open the bathroom door, but found it locked. She struck the door angrily a number of times with her fist as she called out to Said, "What are you doing inside? Open the door!"

Said opened the door without delay, and Amal groaned when she saw his bald head. "What have you done to yourself?" she asked in a fury.

Said collapsed in the chair, and said to Amal in a soft and trembling voice, "I didn't want to upset you with the bad news, for the treatment of cancer starts with chemotherapy, which weakens the hair and causes it to fall off gradually. I preferred to get rid of it all at once."

"You have cancer!" Amal screamed. "Why didn't I know about it?"

"The doctors discovered my condition four weeks ago," Said answered, "and I have only six months left, which will be like a long honeymoon."

Now Raghid said to Said in a voice that Amal did not hear, "What kind of crappy love is this? You torture her with false news and feel no shame in front of your miserable self?"

Then Walid said to Said, "Look at her. What you've done to her does not speak of love."

Said said to both, "Your criticism is valid. I welcome it and will correct it immediately."

"Get angry and curse me if you like," he said to Amal, "for I was doubtful of your love and I told this lie about cancer to find out if I had a place in your heart."

"If you don't have cancer, why did you shave your head?"

"I was called up for the army."

"And there you'll be killed and they won't be able to find your corpse to bury you," Amal said in a trembling voice.

"God forgive you, Amal. You speak as though we were in the old days of the great general Khalid Ibn al-Walid (God bless his soul!). In modern wars, no harm comes to soldiers. They put on their camouflage, walk about in the souks or march in military parades followed by respectful gazes, and are ready for a photograph or a television camera at a moment's notice."

"You must compensate me for the terror that your lying made me feel."

He embraced her, bringing her down to the floor and said he would immediately pay whatever compensation

he owed. Raghid and Walid hid their faces out of jealousy
and embarrassment, and all three men quickly forgot their
differences and were united into one man running around
in a garden picking roses and eating fruit until he was full.
He did not leave, but kept reeling about in its pathways
riotously.

48

Malek and Abdel Qader lived together in something resembling a house and shared the monthly rent without any problems, for they had been born in the same village, had loved the same young woman, experienced the same humiliations, been subject to the same contempt, graduated from the same university, and faced the same unemployment.

One rainy morning Abdel Qader awoke from his sleep, his indignant face expressing revulsion over his old and threadbare socks. He said to Malek that even though it was raining he was going to the souk to buy a new pair of socks, and Malek asked him in a merry voice to buy him a desirable woman. Abdel Qader said, "Malek, my brother, don't ask for what I can't do. The woman who appeals to me may not appeal to you."

"Don't argue," said Malek. "I'm confident the woman who pleases you will please me as well."

Abdel Qader smiled and said, "I'll try to buy you a woman beyond compare."

"I want one with fair skin."

"She will be whiter than pharmacy cotton, and her whiteness will turn rosy red when she feels happy, angry, or embarrassed."

"And I want her to have long black hair."

"Her hair will be as black as charcoal. And if she turns out to be a blonde, I'll order her to dye it black."

"I want her flesh to be cool in summer and warm in winter. And I want her to laugh as though there were no sorrow in the world. And I want her so obedient that if I said there was no water in the sea she would immediately believe that all seas are dry."

Abdel Qader laughed and said, "If I should run into such a woman, I'll forget about all my friends and buy her for myself."

"Don't lie," Malek said confidently. "You're not one of those men who betray a friend for a woman."

Abdel Qader promised to buy the most beautiful woman he could find, and Malek pretended to be pleased and said to Abdel Qader, cautioning, "Make sure you don't choose one of the kind that bites."

Abdel Qader was away for several hours in the souk buying the new socks he needed, but he did not buy a woman. "All the women in the souk were for short-term loan and not for sale," he said to Malek. "Anyone who takes a look at them will be struck with headaches and nausea."

"I changed my mind while you were away," said Malek. "I decided to buy a television set with a big, wide screen. It will be more entertaining."

Malek was not just babbling. A few days later he acquired a television set with a small screen, and Abdel Qader said, "You go ahead and spend the evening enjoying your TV, and I'll spend it in pleasant conversation with my socks. Tomorrow morning we'll find out whose evening was more entertaining."

Malek lay back in his room watching what there was to see on the small screen, and in a few hours found himself struggling against a drowsiness that made his eyelids heavy. He imagined he had been handcuffed, his eyes and mouth taped shut, and surrounded by people who had come out of the screen. They stood around and started rebuking him angrily: "The programs opened with the national anthem. Why did you yawn and not stand up respectfully?"

An announcer with a beard reproached him, "Why didn't you listen to the holy Qur'an rather than keeping yourself busy watching a fly?"

In an accusing voice a heavyset female announcer said, "Weren't you ashamed to smile ironically every time you heard a word about women's rights?"

A comic actor said contemptuously, "Who do you think you are that you didn't laugh when I was acting?"

A female singer asked in surprised tones, "Are you a wall? I sing till my voice goes hoarse but you never show pleasure by dancing!"

What Malek had imagined made his eyes open wide, and he intently watched the news, which showed a scene of soldiers firing at children marching in an angry demonstration. He imagined that a stray bullet had hit him in the chest and thrown him to the ground, and he groaned in pain and terror. He checked his breast with trembling fingers, but there was no wound and no blood dripping from his fingers. He wondered why he should still feel pain, and his hand leaped to turn off the television. Yet he continued to see soldiers descending with their swords upon the necks of men, women and children, and setting on fire green trees, which could not cry out for help.

49

The Inner Neighborhood and the Outer Neighborhood were located side by side. They shared one souk, one coffee house, and one mosque, but their history was marked by continual hatred and conflict. A new feud sprang up between them when some of the men from the Inner Neighborhood spread rumors that the women of the Outer Neighborhood beat their men hard until they cried out for help. The men of the Outer Neighborhood immediately responded by spreading rumors that the women of the Inner Neighborhood received their lovers in the presence of their husbands. The men of the Inner Neighborhood became exceedingly angry, for what was being said touched on their manhood and their honor and could not be ignored, and their response was not going to be simply with words. The two neighborhoods were like a time bomb, and no one knew when it would explode. Some sensible women from both areas rushed to meet secretly. They were discussing the difference between the two neighborhoods at length when Umm Adnan, the most famous old woman from the Inner Neighborhood, suddenly asked, "Is it true that you beat your men if they disobey your orders or if they fall short in their performance at night?"

The women of the Outer Quarter sighed in sadness and said loudly they wished they could beat their husbands. Then they whispered among themselves and smiled cunningly. Umm Adnan said to them, "I'm not stupid. Go ahead and ask what you want to ask without shame or embarrassment."

One of them then asked in a hesitant voice, "Is it true that your women sleep in bed with their lovers while the husbands sleep on the floor?"

Umm Adnan slapped her cheeks in despair and said with a voice dripping with anger, "All the men of our neighborhood and your neighborhood – who among them is a good lover? They're all good for nothing."

With great clamor all the women agreed to work immediately to get rid of all hostility between the men of the two neighborhoods. They went back to their homes and tried to convince their men by night that the conflict between the two neighborhoods was nothing more than a simple misunderstanding which could happen even among brothers. Their success was dazzling, for in a few months some of their bellies started to grow. A new and different rumor then spread, which claimed that the men of the Outer Neighborhood beat their wives, and they did not complain but rather bought canes as presents for their husbands so that their hands and feet would not get tired from all that beating, slapping and kicking. The rumors also claimed that the men of the Inner Neighborhood brought their sweethearts to their homes, and their wives hastened to welcome them, helping them off with their clothes and cooking them the most delicious meals. The wives would then disappear and not come back until they were asked for again.

As soon as these rumors took hold and were treated as facts, calm descended upon the two neighborhoods and the knives, daggers, and clubs that had been made ready for bloody battle were put away. The neighborhoods were then paid a surprise visit by a respectable foreign dignitary who presented himself as the Secretary General of the United Nations. He was welcomed and was allowed to sponsor the historic event at which the peace and friendship treaty between the two neighborhoods was signed. He was also given permission to make an announcement to the correspondents of satellite television stations in which he praised these neighborhoods, considering them forerunners of the peaceful manner in which all future crises in the world would be solved. He declared that as soon as he retired he would spend the rest of his life here and would live in a house half of which was in the Inner Neighborhood and the other half in the Outer. The two neighborhoods were happy to hear this news and felt proud of the exceptional position they had achieved among the nations of the earth. Their harmony grew until they became almost one neighborhood. But then a sudden change took hold of the men in both neighborhoods. The men of the Inner started looking for companions from other neighborhoods, relying on help from their wives who dreamed of long nights in which there would be nothing to do but sleep, and the men of the Outer started beating their wives morning and night.

50

Bahija went into al-Walid hospital heavy with care, wishing her husband were there with her. But he had died a few weeks earlier and missed out on seeing children clinging to his legs.

The nurse gave her the good news that she had given birth to a boy, and Bahija forgot her labor pains and asked the nurse to let her see him immediately. She held him gently and lovingly and called him Bahjat. "Isn't Bahjat a beautiful name?" she asked.

The nurse laughed as she set the baby down in a nearby crib. "A beautiful name," she answered, "but I prefer modern ones."

Bahija could not keep her eyes away from her son and felt that every look made her happiness deeper. In a while she found she had to doze, but she woke up suddenly when she heard a high-pitched, indignant voice cursing all nurses, doctors and hospitals. She was astonished to find that the source of that irate and damning voice was none other than her son. She gasped in amazement, and Bahjat turned to her and smiled as though he had known her for millions of years. "Couldn't you find anything better in this town," he asked in pitying tones, "than this crappy hospital?"

Bahija muttered something in confusion and anguish, and Bahjat said, "As I've observed, this hospital is not free, and it's the duty of those who work here to look after their patients day and night. Yet they left you alone for several hours without a nurse or a doctor looking in on you. You shouldn't keep quiet about this neglect. He who takes our money – we have the right to take his soul."

"You can talk!?" Bahija exclaimed.

Bahjat said, as if insulted, "Not only can I talk, but I can also read, write, and count from one to ten, and I won't be needing any schools or universities."

At that moment, Bahija heard a noise by the door. She thought someone was about to come in and said to her son, "Keep quiet. Don't speak even one word."

Bahjat said, "You're now talking like our leaders."

"If the people here at the hospital discover you can speak," Bahija said, "do you know what might happen? Even I don't know, but my heart doesn't feel at ease. It tells me I might lose you, and I don't know exactly how they'll treat you."

Bahjat laughed again and said, "You won't lose me unless I marry a woman who hates mothers-in-law."

"Pretend you can't talk, just like other children, and you'll find that silence is useful. A silent person sees more than one who talks."

Bahjat promised his mother he wouldn't talk any more and said, "Before I shut up, I want to tell you my father visited me while you were sleeping and congratulated me on my safe arrival. He'll visit you whenever you fall asleep."

She bombarded him with questions, but he kept his promise and did not talk, even after they had left the hospital and were at home by themselves.

When one year had passed, Bahija said to Bahjat, "The time has come for you to start talking like other children."

But Bahjat did not talk and paid no heed to his mother's pleading. All her efforts to get him to talk met with failure. He stuck to his silence, even when he reached the age of twenty. He looked for work, but found no one who would employ a speechless person. All available jobs were suitable only for chatterers. His mother comforted him, saying, "We're not in need of any work. Your father left us with more than enough."

One Friday afternoon Bahjat went into a mosque without having performed ritual ablution. He joined some men relaxing on soft, thick carpets flooded by lights from chandeliers with many lamps. They sat silently and piously in a circle around a corpulent old man with an unkempt beard who was talking about men and women riding together on buses. He said with vehemence and severity that it was forbidden because men would be tempted to indulge in fornication. Bahjat let out a merry laugh which was met with disapproval. He could no longer hold his tongue and found himself compelled to speak. He asked the old man in a loud voice, "Is making love forbidden, master?"

The old man was taken aback, but he smiled as he muttered, "They are unbelievers with reprehensible morals!"

Bahjat then said in a sarcastic tone, "We have believed, and now it's an article of faith with us that riding buses is forbidden. Is riding donkeys at night also forbidden, or is it permitted?"

The old man then recited in a dignified voice a verse from the Qur'an, "God has made unbelief, immorality, and disobedience odious to you. As for those who act wantonly, their resting place will be the flames."

"I asked some questions," Bahjat said angrily, "and I have a right to get answers."

One of the men said in a commanding voice, "Ask questions that benefit your Muslim brethren."

Bahjat thought for some moments, then said, "I have a question for the master. Is it true, Master, that the non-believer Napoleon had only one testicle when he occupied Muslim Egypt?"

The old man said in a scolding and contemptuous manner, "Behave, boy!"

Bahjat faced the men sitting near him and said, "You're asking for honey from a ferret, and expecting to be guided by someone who sees a tall and broad man as a boy. God save you and us from what happens to boys!"

The old man became angry, and those who admired him, his seekers, supporters, and students, were also angry. They attacked Bahjat in a group, descending upon him with their shoes. He resisted, telling them to stop beating him because his blood might stain the precious carpets. They dragged him to the courtyard of the mosque and continued hitting him until he fainted. Then, together they picked him up and threw him outside.

When Bahjat woke up from his faint, he hailed a taxi and asked the driver to take him home. Once there, he tried to speak with his mother and the police, to let them know what had happened. But he couldn't utter even one word, and died a few days later from his wounds. Bahija felt like a combination of widow and orphan. Her house was full of women offering condolence, and she heard some of them whisper something about her son's muteness. She was about to talk back and tell them at length about her son who talked in his cradle, but she changed her mind and with quick steps put some distance between herself and them, as though they were rotting corpses. Thereafter, Bahija slowly cast off all words, and every time she sank deep into silence she was given the opportunity to see her son groveling in the dirt, crying from the fatal wounds he had received on his head. But her silence instantly gave her son enough strength to bear his pain. He would go altogether beyond it, wipe his tears, and run over desert sands where no sun rose, no moon showed itself, and no stars glittered. He would not lose his way or strength, and would carry on running fast so that he might one day soon reach his mother and throw himself into her arms, a baby born a second time without the pangs of a difficult childbirth.

51

I left my house early in the morning without washing my face in cold water, as I usually do. One of my neighbors stopped me and asked as he cast an inquisitive eye on me, "Has the water in your house been shut off because your bill was overdue?"

The grocer asked as he poured the sugar I had ordered in a paper bag, "Why haven't you eaten breakfast? Have you forgotten that to protect your health you must start the day on a full stomach?"

The butcher said as he cut the red meat into small pieces as I had requested, "You're making a mistake because you let your wife go too far in insulting you. The more you ignore her insults, the less she will respect you."

The baker said as he weighed the bread I had ordered, "Reading with a faint light before sleeping is harmful to the eyes."

The vegetable vendor said as he took the money for the vegetables I had bought, "How could you not get angry at your wife's frostiness in bed last night? If I were her husband, I would've divorced her right away."

A black dog said as he busily dug into a pile of rubbish, "In a few hours you'll go to work. Your boss will insult you, and you'll be too scared to talk back."

I did not appreciate the dog's interference in something that did not concern him, and gave him a hard kick. He barked as he scampered off in pain, but did not run away as I had expected and prepared to attack me. So I hurried out of there and went home to put away the things I had bought. There, I decided not to go to work that day so as to enjoy the absence my wife, who had gone away for three days to visit her family. I went into my favorite room and sat at a table made of wood over which white papers were scattered. I imagined I had written on the white paper that it was raining, and all of a sudden it started thundering and heavy rains fell. I also imagined that cats could fly, and suddenly my black cat flew around the room, not hiding his annoyance. He almost crashed into the light bulb dangling from the end of a wire attached to the ceiling. "Can't you see I'm writing?" I said reproachfully. "Keep still and stop making all this noise so I can carry on writing before the words fly from my head."

"What could you be writing?" asked the cat as he settled on the surface of the table. "You're not a student or a writer."

"I'm trying to write a story about Hitler and Abla," I answered.

"Three's no such thing as Hitler and Abla," the cat said. "There is Hitler and Eva, and Antar and Abla."

I was full of admiration for the cultural level of my cat. "Where did you get your education?" I asked. "Which school was it?"

"God save us!" The cat exclaimed, shocked. "If I'd gone to school I would've forgotten how to fly."

I went back to my writing. "What are you writing now?" The cat asked.

"I'm writing a story about Hitler and Abla," I answered. "And don't accuse me of ignorance. I put Hitler in place of Antar for a reason. As soon as the story is published, the critics will see it as a portrait of the clash of European and Arab cultures. Every culture has its own values."

I heard no comment from my cat. I looked at him to find out why, and found him sleeping. I took up my pen as I take hold of a spoon, proceeding like someone who was about to write thousands of words without stopping. The cat opened its eyes and asked, "Are you going to write about me?"

"I'm going to write a novel," I said, "whose title will be *Abu Hashem's Lamp*, and thus far I haven't got beyond the title, but its subject is still cooking on a slow fire."

"But your title," said the black cat, "is stolen from a famous novel whose title is *Umm Hashem's Lamp*."

"What I'm going to write will be the second part of that novel," I said, "completing what the dead writer had started."

My cat said as he yawned, "I'm sure if the writer were alive today and knew of your intention to write such a story, he would die instantly."

I waved a wooden ruler about, threatening the cat, but he flew away towards the window overlooking the garden. "Open this window a little," he said. "The air in this room is stifling. We're going to suffocate."

"Do you think I'm stupid?" I asked. "I open the window, and you fly away and never come back."

I imagined he was staring at me, admiring my cleverness. After a few moments of silence, I said, "Are you angry because I didn't open the window for you?"

"And why should I be angry?" he asked in surprise. "If I fly out into the garden, a bird can swoop down and eat me."

I looked at him fully, admiring his concern for safety, but I suddenly became aware he was staring at the white papers on the table, looking puzzled. I asked what the matter was, and he said, "You talk a lot about what you're writing, but in front of you the paper has remained blank, without even one word. Are you writing with an invisible ink, or is it that you haven't written anything and are satisfied to talk about what you would like to write but haven't yet written?"

"You're talking like a detective now," I said, jesting, "and not like a friend who's with me day and night."

I sat back, deep into something that resembled thought, and my black cat came near and asked inquisitively what I was thinking about. I answered that I was thinking about the future, and he asked, "In the future, do you intend to buy a gun to hunt down the fish that will damage the garden by jumping from tree to tree?"

I said, "I'm thinking that in the future scientists may succeed in inventing a mysterious box with an illuminated screen on which people will appear moving and talking."

"Are you mocking me?" the cat asked in anger. "What you're talking about has already been invented. It's the television. But you haven't bought one because you're cheap."

"If I'd bought one," I answered, "it would've drawn me away from you and prevented me from talking with you and keeping you company."

The cat was silent for a few moments, then suddenly said, "I'll buy you a set, even if I have to ask for a loan from Somalia."

"I didn't know you loved me that much," I said to the cat with a trembling voice.

"It seems you forgot I was a cat," he said, mocking, "and that cats don't love anyone."

I was angry for a minute or two and said nothing. Then, I took up the conversation with my cat again. I begged him to go wandering around in the homes of the neighbors and listen to their secrets, then come back and tell me what they were saying, that I may get some amusement and be saved from a boredom that was about to kill me. To my surprise, the cat became angry and said, his tail thrashing, that he wasn't an informer or gossip monger.

"Are you content to have me die of boredom?" I asked.

"Go out for a while," the cat said. "Who's keeping you locked up in the house?"

"Where shall I go?" I asked.

"Visit your friends," he said.

"And where are these friends?" I asked.

"Go to a coffee house," said the cat.

"It's not my custom to sit around in coffee houses," I said.

"Wander about in the streets," said the cat.

"Loitering requires strong legs, which I don't have," I said.

The cat took pity on me, and was about to set out for the neighbors' houses. I asked him to take particular care to get news of men who were like fire and beautiful women who were like butterflies. He came back in a few hours to tell me at length about a female cat as white as snow, whose meowing was more beautiful than music. I told him I was sick and couldn't get out of bed to call a doctor, and asked him to call one right away before I died. "You die," the cat said, "and I'll gobble you up slowly."

I ordered him to stop joking, and he asked, "What shall I say to the doctor? Meow, meow?"

"Speak with him as you're talking with me right now," I said.

"Every cat is permitted to talk only to one person in his lifetime," the cat said. "Sadly, I chose one who's short-lived, and I won't be able to talk to anyone else after your death."

"Since I'm going to die," I said, "I must share my wealth with the poor."

"Quiet," said the cat. "Keep quiet, and don't let me die of laughter."

"And I must say goodbye to my family and relatives," I said.

"You're the last living person in your family," the cat said.

"It's not proper that I should die without seeing my wife," I said.

"There's no reason to see her," said the cat. "She might let out trills of joy."

"And who will bury me?" I asked the cat.

"Have you forgotten you won't be needing a funeral or a grave," said the cat, "because I'm going to gobble you up and invite my friends to join in with me?"

I then closed my eyes and died and waited for the cats' teeth, hoping they would be strong enough to tear cold flesh apart.

52

Shukri al-Nimr left the grounds of the school where he had been a teacher for several years and set out for his home. He was surprised to find a white piece of paper attached to the kitchen door in which his wife informed him that her mother was sick and she had gone to visit her. She directed him to take the food out of the refrigerator and heat it before eating. He ignored her advice and wandered about in the space of his small house feeling weary. He imagined he was asking his students to write a composition about a school teacher married to a childless widow whom he loved. Feeling bored with staying all alone in the house, he went out into a noisy street crowded with people where he saw an old woman who looked very much like his mother making ready to cross. He tried to help her, but she hit him on the head with her handbag and accused him of wanting to steal it. He then remembered his shameful neglect of his mother, whom he had not seen in several years. He rushed to visit her grave at the cemetery and stood close enough to touch it, his head bowed. "Did you get married?" his mother asked.

He told her he was married, and she asked, "How many children do you have?"

"Only one," he said in a faint voice.

"Don't lie," she said.

"I don't have any children," he said.

"Who's the lazy one?" she asked. "You or your wife?"

He left the graveyard without saying goodbye to his mother and tried to get on a bus, but the conductor would not let him board. Even though most of the seats were empty, he claimed the bus was full and told him to take another one. Shukri then cursed all buses and their inventors and walked until he reached home, showing obvious signs of fatigue. He found his wife laughing and speaking with children who could not be seen. He asked about her sick mother and she said, "I don't think she'll pull through this time."

She said to the children, "There, come say hello to daddy."

He went along with her. He pretended there were children there breaking into joyful cries, and he went to sleep to the din of their voices gradually receding from his ears.

When Shukri al-Nimr woke up in the morning, the house was as quiet as a grave. His wife was in the kitchen wearing black clothes, drinking coffee and weeping. She asked him to wear clothes of the same color as hers and said, "Hurry, so we won't be late for mother's funeral."

He put on his clothes without delay and asked the invisible children to eat their breakfast quickly so as not to be late for school.

53

Fathi was hungry and bought two apples, one red and the other green. He went to a nearby park, sat on a bench, and was about to bite into the green. "Am I going to be executed without trial?" the apple asked.

"You're not more valuable than a human being," Fathi answered.

"Am I not even allowed to write my will?" asked the apple.

"I won't eat you," Fathi said. "I don't want to be accused of hostility toward green apples."

Fathi was about to bite into the red apple, but it said in a threatening voice: "If you eat me, you'll regret it."

"May God save us from regret!" exclaimed Fathi.

"I'm certain you're ignorant of who I am," the red apple said, "and you don't know from what quarter aid will come."

"Are you a member of the ruling party, or the opposition?" Fathi asked in disbelief.

"Are you also going to ask me about my relation to drug smuggling and distribution?" the red apple asked back.

"Is your brother an officer in the army?" Fathi asked.

"Have you ever heard of apples that carry arms and kill?" the apple answered.

"Is your uncle a minister?" asked Fathi.

"There are no government employees in my family," the red apple answered. "The work that trees do has nothing to do with laws, commands, and decisions."

"Is your uncle one of those who wear a large turban?" Fathi asked.

"A question like that," the apple answered, "should not be addressed to red apples."

"Is one of your relatives a millionaire then?" asked Fathi.

The red apple answered, "There is no record in history of a single apple tree going into a bank."

Fathi laughed, a quick mocking chuckle. He ate the red apple and then the green and paid no heed to their loud cries of complaint. He wiped his lips with a paper napkin and threw it away, and the napkin complained about people who show no gratitude.

54

An old woman whose back was bent went into a park whose trees were bare. She stood in front of the immense stone statue of a tall man with a stern face, his right hand raised in a gesture that inspired awe and respect, as if blessing his invisible minions kneeling there. The old woman was filled with an overwhelming fear that made her weak in the legs. She wanted to look daggers at the man who had killed her sons and their father, but her gaze was incapable of letting go of its usual sadness and humility. The old woman felt as if she were shrinking. She continued to shrink until she disappeared, and everything around her – the buildings and the people – also began to shrink, until they too disappeared. Nothing remained except the statue, and the birds whose pleasure it was to crap upon it.

55

What happened to him was beyond belief. He ate (God preserve him!) a citizen without knowing he was a talented poet. His character changed, and he became (God preserve him!) an innovative poet in spite of the fact that before he couldn't tell the difference between a cheek and the bottom of the foot.

What happened to him was beyond belief. Every time he devoured one of us (God preserve him!) he delivered a funeral oration in words as black as charcoal and exuding so much grief they sprinkled salt on water.

What happened to him (God preserve him!) was beyond belief, and what happened to us was beyond belief also. The one stuffed with our flesh and crying over our dead bodies was but one person, and we wouldn't have needed to fire a gun twice. But we didn't fire even one shot because the undernourished dogs that are always in flight barked in warning that the enemy was approaching fast, and he (God preserve him!) and his men with the proud mustaches, their bodies weighed down by the weapons they were carrying, ran with terrified steps to hide their heads under their pillows, giving no thought to what was going to happen to the rest of their bodies. They ignored the rough hands that stripped them of their clothes, for the act of being straddled did not diminish their pleasure at having saved their necks from being stained with blood. On the contrary they welcomed it as a foundation for a larger human family, and spread rumors to the effect that the brutal soldiers of the enemy were beautiful women in disguise. A magnificent delight spread over air, sea, and land. At that moment his ears (God preserve him!) grew bigger, and he could hear the people's voices rising toward the sky, praying it would grace them with a few drops of water. He (God preserve him!) listened to their prayers and released his strange rain over them. The moment a drop of it came in contact with a man's head it bored a hole in it and sucked up all that was inside, turning it into a skull whose owner had been dead for a thousand years. The people were terrified and raised their voices to the heavens, asking to be saved from what had befallen them, and he (God preserve him!) had a long, merry laugh until his eyes filled with tears and he ordered his minions to remind people that the sky to which they were appealing was nothing more than a wide-open blue space that was deaf and mute and that they had nothing else to turn to but him (God preserve him!), for he alone was the powerful one who could answer prayers and come to the rescue. The big tribes rushed to sing his praises and exalt him (God preserve him!), but not our small tribe, which was out of favor and always subject to ridicule. Its land was taken, its wealth stolen, and its women scattered under those who raped them. Our tribe became the laughing stock of all the others, and we swore revenge, even after a million years, in order to get back our land and wealth and wipe away the shame brought upon our women. But we were unarmed and weak, with fear instead of blood running deep in our veins.

We cried for many years and sought help from him who
alone was the source of relief, and he sent us invisible armies
bringing the most modern weapons. We examined them
with admiration and pleasure, and as soon as we touched
them our bodies lost their weakness and terror and became
strong and muscular, fearing no one. We welcomed what
had happened to us and lost no time in opening a market,
more like a small village, specializing in the selling of arms.
Its reputation spread among the tribes, and the number of
customers grew. We joined the famous and wealthy and no
longer asked for anything other than long life. Our secret
efforts were crowned with success. We obtained a written
promise that we wouldn't die, and we sold our graves and
the graves of our forefathers and grandchildren for the
most exorbitant prices, and became an envied example
among the tribes.

56

Ali al-Tayyib woke up from a coma that had lasted several years and transformed him into an ugly old man whose back was bent and whose skin was baggy, one who walked wearily leaning on his cane with a shaky hand and skinny fingers. When he came home from the hospital he had entered as a young man powerful as thunder, he welcomed many of his relatives, who had rushed to his house to congratulate him on having been saved from a very baffling illness. He made sure to ask them insistently and in detail about their personal circumstances until he knew what had befallen them during his absence. Then he asked many questions that had nothing to do with their lives, and their answers were quick and to the point.

The sun still rose every morning, and one full day was still a day and a night. Summer was still long and hot and winter long and cold.

The President of the Republic still held his position. He had not been replaced, nor had he changed. He had become increasingly more healthy and youthful, and had resolved to walk in the funeral processions of all his citizens as well as those of their children and grandchildren.

The Prime Minister had not been replaced, and he had not changed. He still jogged ten miles every day.

The Speaker of the Parliament had not been replaced, and he had not changed. He had recently divorced his three wives and replaced them with someone not yet twenty.

The Foreign Minister had not been replaced, and he had not changed. He remained the most esteemed minister.

The Minister of Defense had not been replaced, and he had not changed. He was now in a position to buy several banks.

The Minister of Trade had not been replaced, and he had not changed. His hobby was still to own precious rugs without having to pay.

The Minister of Information had not been replaced, and he had not changed. He still talked day and night.

The Minister of Culture had not been replaced, and he had not changed. Before it died, culture had granted him everything it owned.

The Minister of Health had not been replaced, and he had not changed. His health was just fine, and he might catch a cold every ten years.

The Minister of Education had not been replaced, and he had not changed. But there were serious rumors to the effect that he would be replaced in a hundred years.

The Minister of the Interior had not been replaced, and he had not changed. How could he change when the sun itself did not change?

Ali al-Tayyib then asked his relatives about a coffee house he used to frequent and was told it had been torn down and was now part of a broad avenue that was teeming with speeding cars. He asked about a journalist whose daring he held in high regard and was told he had opened a shoe repair shop. He asked about his favorite actress and was told she had died of cancer. He asked about a dancer he admired and was told she had gotten old and had taken to wearing a headscarf. He asked about a singer whose music used to move him and was told he was now devoting himself to commercial advertisements. He asked about a poet whose poetry he used to memorize and was told he had committed suicide. He asked about a river and was told it had dried up. Ali al-Tayyib then closed his eyes and tried to get back into his coma, but his efforts were not successful.

57

As he walked with heavy steps out of a bar Kamil al-Mihsal was arrested in the middle of the night and accused of being an important member of a secret religious organization that was responsible for many assassinations. He felt fear and surprise at the same time, but his surprise got the better of his fear, and he laughed and laughed until slaps, blows, and kicks descended upon him. He begged his interrogators to ask about him and his way of life, for he had never once gone into a mosque. He gambled and got drunk every night, had to be carried home, and had no concern in life other than chasing and winning beautiful women. But the interrogators mocked his explanations, claiming they were nothing more than a very craftily designed mask behind which he hid in order to commit the ugliest deeds.

Kamil al-Mihsal spent many months between life and death in the dungeons of the interrogators, where he was pressed to disclose what he did not know and had no connection with, and was then left in prison for many years until he was convinced he would get out only after he was dead.

Unexpectedly, the government came to a secret agreement with clandestine religious organizations and started to release their members from prison, but no one paid any attention to Kamil al-Mihsal. He complained, protested, and pleaded, but was told contemptuously and firmly that he was a debauched non-believer and had no connection with religion and politics and therefore could not benefit from the formal accord just reached. He was angry and decided to escape, and did escape from a prison which no one had been able to escape from before. His fellow prisoners were envious because he would now be able to breathe fresh air not as a prisoner but as a free man. The official agencies in charge went absolutely mad. They considered what had taken place a challenge to their authority and a diminution of its awe-inspiring power. They issued orders to have him arrested again and brought back to his cell beaten and broken and bound up with the heaviest of shackles. Their merciless men spread like excited wasps in search of him. They broke into homes at night and interrogated anyone who was thought to have any connection with Kamil al-Mihsal, but they never succeeded in catching him. It seemed he had evaporated. Of course he was not water that can evaporate but was so brilliant at disguise that even his own mother would not have been able to recognize him. If he had stopped her in the street and said he was her son she would have denied it angrily and hostilely. He could also forge whatever papers and official documents he needed, and had enough money to live comfortably, feeling at ease in the world outside a prison which now appeared novel, attractive, ambiguous, savage, and confusing, and worthy of being taken by storm.

The official agencies in charge despaired of catching Kamil al-Mihsal and circulated rumors that claimed he had either fled to a foreign country or had been secretly murdered by partners in crime whom he had betrayed. Yet Kamil al-Mihsal was not murdered and did not emigrate, but lived well-disguised in his own country. He met by chance a woman whom he loved and respected, and he married her and became a father to a son who, when he had grown up, broke into a military barracks to steal weapons. He was sentenced to ten years and was a model prisoner who never complained or pleaded, feeling the same love for his cell as he would for the home in which was born, and every time he saw himself in his sleep wandering around freely in the streets he woke up in terror, as though he were walking in his own funeral.

58

Many armed men descended at dawn upon the home of Farid al-Murabba', yanked him out of bed, and took him in his pyjamas to a hospital that had been closed down and used as an interrogation center. There they threw him down at the feet of an interrogator with disheveled hair, wearing white underclothes that were dirty. He was yawning and rubbing his eyes as though he had just been awakened for an urgent matter that could not wait. Farid was accused of refusing to be bribed, and he looked around with curiosity, searching for whoever it was who would not be bribed, but the interrogator slapped him and said, "Don't act stupid. We have determined you're the one who refuses to be bribed and who is an enemy of those who give bribes as well as receive them."

Farid al-Murabba' gasped in shock and wasted no time in denying the accusation, insisting that he came from a family where no one refused the blessing of a bribe.

Farid told his interrogator that he was famous for obeying his parents, that his mother had counseled him on her deathbed not to refuse any bribes, and that his father threatened to disown him if he ever heard any gossip about him to the effect that he refused a bribe no matter how small, urging him to remember that an intelligent man accepts a small bribe as a bridge to larger ones and that small and insignificant sins lead to big and noble ones.

Farid al-Murabba' said to the interrogator that what he had been accused of was an outright lie, since his relatives, his neighbors, and his friends all accepted bribes. His colleagues at work were also bribable and tried to imitate him but did not succeed because he was so ready to accept bribes at all times that his enviers started calling him "the saw." He added that if he had to live only on his salary he would not be alive now.

Farid al-Murabba' then said to the interrogator that bribery was the adornment of life on earth. It came into being to endure and defeat its dull-witted and short-lived enemies.

All that Farid al-Murabba' admitted did not save him from being tortured for many long days that passed slowly, but he did not change his position that he welcomed bribes and defended bribery. He offered the interrogator a not-insignificant amount of money, with the prospect of it being increased rather than decreased, to be delivered at the beginning of every month. The interrogator then was convinced of his innocence and ordered his release. Farid al-Murabba' returned to his family, who received him as though he had come back from the grave. But his arrest and having that shameful charge leveled at him made it impossible for him to walk among people with his head raised high.

59

A fierce battle broke out between Abdel Majid al-Ruwaili, who made and sold traditional women's robes, and Fuad Sireen, a photographer who complained of not having enough work and became a seller of women's clothes imported from the most fashionable designers in the world. Their battle was the more ferocious because their shops were side by side. Fuad Sireen was confident that his neighbor would certainly operate at a loss because women were tired of traditional robes and were abandoning them and competing in wearing modern dresses. Abdel Majid al-Ruwaili did not surrender but urged the imam of the local mosque to play his part in protecting praiseworthy morals, which would be lost if women were to let go of their traditional robes. The imam sighed with sadness and was content merely to say that speech was of no use if people did not have ears to listen. Abdel Majid then talked to many men and urged them to make their women wear traditional clothes so that vice would not prevail. They agreed with enthusiasm, but their wandering eyes convinced him that women had now become the keepers of the men. He despaired and made only a small number of robes, spending most of his time sitting quietly in front of his shop looking serious and eyeing sadly the crowds of women who went into his neighbor's shop. It seemed the battle between the two neighbors had ended in a sweeping victory for Fuad Sireen, for what he sold was very popular and realized huge profits, while those who came into his neighbor's shop were only old women who bargained for days and spent not a piaster until they had squeezed the soul out of the seller. Yet within a few months Fuad Sireen was surprised that fewer and fewer women were coming into his shop. His merchandise was not moving, and no one was more responsible for that than his neighbor Abdel Majid al-Ruwaili, who no longer made and sold traditional robes but became an expert in the manufacture and replication of fashionable garments. He hastened to copy and sell at a very low price any foreign garment that came on the market. He claimed that imported clothes were made for quick consumption and women would be forced to replace them with new ones because they did not last more than a few months. He, on the other hand, made a dress that did not force a woman to buy new a one unless she was rich and a spendthrift. He made sure to copy only those garments with the most prestigious international labels.

Fuad Sireen tried to advise people that imitation merchandise could not possibly be of the same quality as the original, but no one listened because low prices can offer more persuasive arguments. He found himself obliged to admit he had lost the battle with his neighbor. He had to give up the import business and buy clothes from Abdel Majid al-Ruwaili instead. He welcomed his defeat as his profits increased, and started planning with partners for the smuggling of al-Ruwaili's merchandise into the countries that designed and exported fashionable clothes.

60

No one hated Omar al-Dakar, for he was modest and cheery, and took advantage of his profession as a policeman to help those who had been detained, secretly giving them lessons in the kind of wily and duplicitous testimony it would be best to give during interrogation to avoid torture or having to remain in prison for long periods. At the same time he served as a postman between detainees and their families.

No one hated Omar al-Dakar, for he was content with his life. Every time someone urged him to do something to make life better for himself and his family like everyone else, he laughed and said, "Praise be to the Creator of tin and gold! Whoever heard that tin could turn into gold, and gold into tin?"

No one hated Omar al-Dakar, but all the furniture he had at home was stolen while he was on duty at the station, his wife was visiting her family, and his children were at school. There was nothing to make the furniture worth stealing. It was old and cheap even when it was new. Omar's investigations did not yield any results. His neighbors said that when they saw the furniture being taken away they thought he was moving without letting them know, and that had made them angry with him.

Omar al-Dakar was surprised a few days later when his wife was also kidnapped. What happened to her was thought to be amazing, for she was no longer a young woman. She was loud and ugly, and was neither wine nor vinegar.

A few weeks later Omar al-Dakar's three children were kidnapped as they were leaving school. This kidnapping appeared stupid, for they were young and had no skills except cursing and swallowing food without ever acknowledging the existence of fullness.

These thefts did not affect Omar al-Dakkar. He kept on laughing, eating voraciously, and sleeping as usual. Rumors circulated – and found those who believed them – that he was the perpetrator, but their falsehood quickly became apparent when Omar al-Dakar was himself kidnapped and disappeared like dust on a rainy day. All those who knew him found this strange, as Omar was lazy and slothful, a voracious eater and a sound sleeper, and afflicted with seven diseases. Yet those who were under arrest in prisons and police stations were the most baffled, for they started giving their interrogators confused testimony that brought them brutal kinds of torture and longer stays in prison than they enjoyed at home. Omar al-Dakar was himself taken aback at what happened to him, for he had become a different kind of policeman. He was now elegant, alert, grim, very harsh, rude, and as cold as death. He lived in a new quarter of town, and his house was full of luxury furniture, the like of which even his superiors did not have. All thieves were afraid of him and were careful to keep him happy, since he knew them one by one, as if he were the midwife that brought them out of their mothers' bellies. He even knew those who were going to become thieves in the future, but he did not object to their practicing their profession as long as they abided by what was agreed – one half of whatever they stole was for them and the other for him, which he received into his hands unflinchingly, repeating that he was born poor but would not die poor.

Omar al-Dakar made no exceptions for anyone. When he caught his son with a book he had stolen from the public library, he rebuked him severely, counted the number of pages in the book, and tore off half of them. And if he caught a deceitful thief who wanted to cheat him, he punished him instantly by increasing his own share of the stolen goods or by taking them all.

One day a thief who was new to the profession dared to complain. "We are the ones who labor," he said, "disobeying God and putting our souls at risk when we steal, and you mistreat us while remaining secure, at ease, and feeling no shame."

Omar smiled scornfully and said to him, "It's a truism that speaking with idiots is fatal. If you were intelligent, you would've kissed my hands and feet, thanking me because I take not only half of what you steal but also half of the sins for which you will be held to account on the Day of harsh Judgment."

Omar became famous for being a man who did not get angry. His wife used to joke with him, counseling him to see a doctor in order to be cured of his coldness and start feeling anger. But he did feel an unremitting anger the day he learned a certain man had sold his house and received payment in cash, and that on his way to deposit it in the bank an armed thief had held him up, robbed him of the money, and run away.

Omar felt an insult that could never be erased. He could not believe there was a thief still alive who could defy him in such an impudent, mean, and low manner and he resolved to search him out and find him, in order to know who he was. Even if the thief had hidden himself under the seventh earth, Omar was determined to teach him a lesson that would make all the other thieves shake with fear when they thought of it. But the thief remained unknown, enjoying the fruits of his thievery. Omar felt a despair that put bargains and pleasures at a distance. He stayed away from food, except on rare occasions, and drank day and night. He did not sleep except after he had swallowed many pills, against the advice of his terrified family. Then he died suddenly in great pain, and the thieves took care to walk unhurriedly and respectfully in his funeral procession, not feeling particularly happy or vengeful, for they knew that any policemen compelled to be absent would immediately be replaced by another. With heads bent, they saw his corpse lowered into the grave wrapped in a soiled white shroud. Afterwards they separated, feeling sorry there was no one among the mourners whom it would proper to rob. Omar then found himself all alone, lying on the humid soil of the grave. He wished he had brought his comfortable cotton-filled pillow. The grave was so dark that a hand, if it could move, would have been able to touch its darkness. Omar said to himself, "This is one more proof that the power company does not distinguish between the living and the dead."

When night came two angels entered the grave without having made an appointment or having asked for permission, and he welcomed them even though he had never seen them before. He apologized for not being able to receive them in the official uniform of a policeman who never disobeyed God, His Prophet, or the government. He asked them how long the procedure of transferring him to Paradise would take. He gave as justification for his question the fact that he had never died before and did not know how things were managed in the other world, stating that Paradise was in need of a policeman with the benefit of long experience like himself. The angels informed him their task was to interrogate him about his life, which had just ended, and would start with a few questions. A scowl came over Omar's face as he said to them in disbelief, "I never imagined the world would come to such a ridiculous turn that I, who have spent all my life asking the questions and listening to the answers, should be obliged to answer them."

Omar refused to answer any questions, but he said he would change his position if they agreed to help him. He asked about the unknown thief who had challenged him on his beat, burying his reputation in the mud. He swore he would answer all their questions if they could tell him the name of that thief. The angels said they had nothing to do with the world of thieves and wouldn't be able to find out his name until he died and they had questioned him. Omar was surprised to hear this and felt great relief, and his face let go of its frown. He said to the two angels, "I now realize how stupid I was when I wanted to identity a thief that even the angels can't identify."

He informed them that he had changed his position out of respect for their visit and promised he would answer their questions on other nights, begging them to consider the current visit as an occasion to get acquainted. But he warned them that his feeble memory made it impossible for him to answer more than half their questions and yawned loudly. He said in a weak and trembling voice that his funeral that day had exhausted him, taking away all his energy. He covered his face with his shroud and slept very deeply, but he woke up very quickly when the first kick landed on his head.

61

Madiha was a woman who used to feel ill at ease whenever she saw two people talking amicably. Exploiting her talent for new and unusual rumors and trickery, she would turn into a snake and never rest until the friends had disagreed and become enemies. At the same time she appeared to her husband, Rabi' al-Saqqal, as nothing but a weak and peaceable woman, attractive with her dark complexion. She was modest and never spoke much, so good-natured that if a cat were to eat her supper her tender heart would not find it in itself to shoe it away.

When her husband's business failed and he declared bankruptcy, she did not leave him but encouraged him to confront his vicious creditors, who left nothing of worth in his shop or home but took possession of it. Some of them threatened him with death, but Madiha answered them boldly. "Killing him would be easy," she said, "but that won't get you your money back. Business means one day you gain, and the next you lose. If he remains alive there's still hope you'll get your money back."

But the most vicious among them, Fahd al-Ramy, was not ready to be convinced by any arguments. He said he preferred to lose a son rather than lose a piaster. He then boldly set about kidnapping Madiha, taking an oath that the hostage wife would not return to her husband until his funds were back in his pocket. He kept her in his own home, where she lived with his wife and three spinster sisters. Rabi' did not resort to the police, for he came from an environment that did not set any store by letting the police take care of crises. He preferred to work through respected middle men, but their beautiful and calm words did not result in al-Ramy's release of Madiha. He insisted that she would remain in his home, honored and well-taken care of, and would go back to her home only when his money came back.

Not a week had passed before al-Ramy was stunned by the change which had taken place in his home as a result of Madiha's well-planned intrigues. He started quarreling with his wife, and she in turn started fighting with his sisters, and the differences among the sisters almost reached a point of their hitting each other with their shoes. Fahmi then realized that if Madiha remained in his house the walls would start quarreling with the ceiling until the whole house collapsed. He rushed to return her to her husband, Rabi' al-Saqqal, with an apology, cursing the anger which made him do embarrassing and foolish things. Rabi' al-Saqqal smiled as he asked, "And the money I owe you?"

Fahd al-Ramy looked around, as though the question were addressed to someone else. "What amount?" he said, pretending surprise. "In my entire life I never loaned you any money. There must be an error in your book-keeping."

Fahd rushed out of the house, and Rabi' gazed at his wife wondering what was going on. He found her the same weak woman to whom he had become accustomed, a woman so gentle that a cat could eat her breakfast, lunch and dinner without her finding the courage to object.

62

Pretending he was seriously interested in what she was saying, Saadi gazed into his wife's face and held back his rage at her open mouth, from which words kept flowing without a break. He was sure that if at that moment he had stabbed her with a knife nothing would have come out of her veins except words that looked like little hedgehogs. She spoke at length about the neighbors, their lies, and their fascination with glittery appearances. She spoke at length about the butcher, who didn't fear God but cheated all his customers. If he sold meat to his own mother he would still have cheated her. And she spoke at length about a cat that prowled the streets. It stole into people's homes and pinched meat set aside for cooking. She fed its kittens only the most tender pieces. The wife praised dogs and insisted they keep a vicious dog who would make it his task to kill the cat. Saadi interrupted, asking her to stay quiet if only for two minutes, and she looked at him reproachfully. "Are my words that offensive?" she asked.

"God save us!" he exclaimed. "Don't misunderstand me. Your words are rich, and the listener needs a break in order to swallow and digest them, and turn them into vitamins that run their course in the body."

"In that case," she said, "since I give you the best nourishment and save you from doctors, you must pay me what you would pay one of them."

"It's true," he said, "I haven't been to a doctor since we got married, but my heart tells me that a doctor will soon visit and examine me, and will decide that I died from a heart attack."

"Haven't they invented something to protect against heart attacks?" she asked.

"Inventions are many," he answered, "but they have yet to invent a drug for someone dying from feeling sick at heart."

At that moment, like an unexpected savior, the telephone rang and Saadi rushed to answer it. He held the receiver close to his ear and spoke with a friend who invited him to get together at a coffee house. Saadi then returned the receiver to its place and told his wife a friend had called from the hospital, where he was taken after a car had run him over and broken his leg and he had no one to look after him.

"What about his wife?" she asked.

"He's not married," he answered.

"How old is he?"

"Thirty, or may be a little less."

"Is he rich?"

"He's not in need."

"What does he do for a living?"

"He doesn't work. He has enough properties to save him having to work."

"And what does he look like?"

"He could be the brother of Suad Husni, may God have mercy on her soul!"

"How much did she leave him?"

"I said he could be her brother, I didn't say he was her brother."

"What do you think of marrying him to my sister In'am? Come, don't waste time in chattering. Go see him in the hospital and speak to him eloquently and intelligently about my sister, her beauty and moral character, and her skill in cooking."

"Should I also tell him about her skill in beating her first husband, who had to spend three days in hospital?"

"Her husband was unbearable and deserved what he got. He used to fall asleep and snore whenever she tried to talk to him. If he'd been my husband, I wouldn't have been satisfied with beating him, I would've killed him."

Utterly stunned, Saadi fell silent, and his wife asked in surprise, "What happened to you? Have you swallowed your tongue?"

Saadi then placed his hands over his ears, pretending to be in great pain, and said to his wife that he could see her lips moving but couldn't hear her voice, and he begged her to hurry and call a doctor.

63

Aref woke up from his customary afternoon nap and shouted at his wife in a demanding voice, "O Raifa, where's the coffee?"

Raifa came speedily into the bedroom and put in front of him a hot cup of coffee from which steam was rising. She told him his mother had called while he slept to let him know his father had a cold and was suffering from a severe cough.

"I hope it turns out well," he said.

He started drinking his coffee slowly and silently. Suddenly he said to Raifa, "Here, tell me what you want. Your eyes betray you when you want to ask for something."

Raifa laughed and asked him to teach her how to drive. His face turned red and he refused her request on the pretext of saving her from unforeseen dangers that threatened her life. She tried to argue but he said in a cutting voice, "Forget the subject. I don't want to hear about it again."

With a scowl on his face, he dressed and left his ninth-floor apartment. He got into his car and drove to his parents' house, where he found his father sleeping and his mother darning old socks. He sat opposite her in silence. When she asked him what the matter was, he told her what Raifa had

189

asked for. "Why the anger?" asked the mother, surprised. "You have a car, and Raifa is smart. She'll learn quickly."

Aref looked at his mother disapprovingly and said, "It's a fact that women have half a brain. A kid does not deceive a billygoat. Today she takes the car and drives it, and tomorrow she'll drive me."

He rushed out of his parent's home and headed for the coffee house without waiting for his father to wake up. He sat with his friends, and, as usual, they started to vie with each other in defaming their wives. He told them what his wife had asked for, and they praised his alert and cautious course of action. But they welcomed warmly the thought of having women less ugly than their wives ride them on their backs.

When Aref became hungry and bored with his friends, he went back home and found his wife turning over the pages of a women's magazine. He snatched it away from her hands and tore it up angrily, saying that magazines like this only spread loose morals and shameless behavior. There was no purpose behind them except to corrupt the wives and daughters of Muslims. Raifa said not a word but rose and reached for the television set. Aref said to her reprovingly, "Don't break the agreement we made the day we bought it. We agreed that it would be turned on only for the news and religious programs, and for recitations from the holy Qur'an. Now they're showing foreign films and local serials. Films are forbidden. Watching the immorality that goes on in them is prohibited, and serials are trivial and do more harm than good."

"How do I entertain myself then?" asked Raifa in a choking voice.

Aref answered, as if amazed, "You can entertain yourself by cleaning the house, washing and ironing clothes, and mopping the floor. Sport and cleanliness at the same time. Didn't I advise you to memorize the holy Qur'an because it would make you feel good, but you only memorized the opening sura. The house is full of books about the lives of saintly men. I'll shave my mustache if you touched any of them even once. God protect us from the women of this age!"

Raifa rushed to the balcony in an attempt to throw herself down from the ninth floor, but Aref stopped her. He reproached her, saying that killing oneself is forbidden by God. She then rushed into the bedroom and threw herself on the bed. He tried to take her hand, but she moved away from him as from a stranger. He reproached her again, and said that God and his Prophet abhorred a woman who did not satisfy her husband's legitimate needs. Raifa then lay on the bed with her legs wide open, feeling certain she would be attempting suicide again.